OCT -- 2016

A Sister's Wish

A Sister's Wish

The Charmed Amish Life, Book Three

Shelley Shepard Gray

AVON

INSPIRE

An Imprint of HarperCollinsPublishers

P.S.™ is a trademark of HarperCollins Publishers.

HarperCollins books may be purchased for educational, business, or sales promotional use. For information please e-mail the Special Markets Department at SPsales@harpercollins.com.

FIRST EDITION

Illustrated map copyright © 2015 by Laura Hartman Maestro

Library of Congress Cataloging-in-Publication Data has been applied for.

ISBN 978-0-06-233783-2

16 17 18 19 20   OV/RRD   10 9 8 7 6 5 4 3 2 1

To my editor, Chelsey Emmelhainz:
If I didn't have you in my corner, I know
I couldn't write books like this.
Thank you for everything.
And thank you again.

The author is grateful for being allowed to reprint the Monster Cookies
recipe from Country Blessings Cookbook by Clara Coblentz.
The Shrock's Homestead
9943 Copperhead Rd. N.W.
Sugarcreek, OH 44681

In thee shall all families of the earth be blessed.

—GENESIS 12:3

Life stops when you stop dreaming.
Hope ends when you stop believing.
Love ends when you stop caring.
Friendship ends when you stop sharing.

—AMISH PROVERB

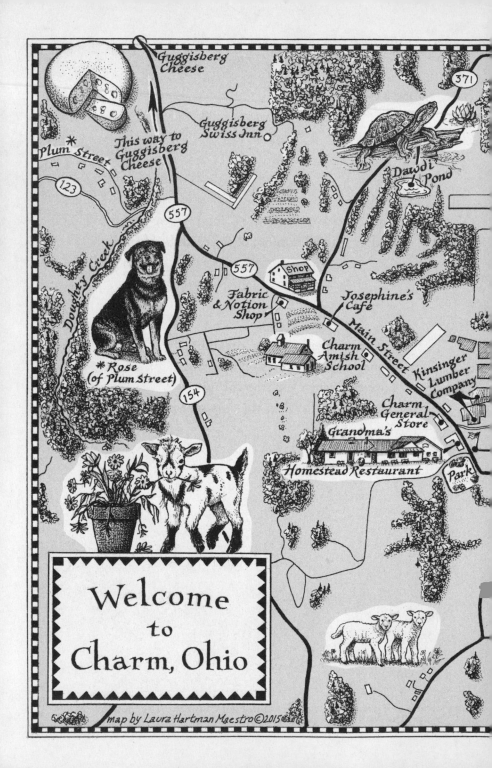

Welcome to Charm, Ohio

map by Laura Hartman Maestro ©2015

371

369

157

369 · the Kinsinger Home

57

Oscar

159

Simon's House

Charm Public School

Bank

70

U.S. Post Office

70

557

Darla's Farm

Walnut Creek

600

159

Many of these locations are real, but like Princess the goat and Oscar the bulldog, Shelley imagined a few, too.

Prologue

Thirteen years ago

He had almost made it.

All he had to do was make it another two miles, then he'd be able to catch the bus to New Philly and eventually Mansfield. After that? Simon Hochstetler reckoned it didn't really matter. He would be free and that was good enough.

But for now, all he had to do was ignore the pain in his side, make it over the next bend, then finally hike through the northern edge of the Kinsingers' property. Once he did all that, the road would be flat. A whole lot easier to walk on.

He winced as he shifted his stuffed army-green backpack on his left shoulder, wishing that his right one wasn't as bruised as it was. 'Course, if he was making wishes, he should probably start with wishing that he didn't have a black eye or cut lip. From there he could wish his ribs weren't hurting, either.

His father had been in fine form tonight.

He walked on, patting his pocket, feeling for the wad of

money he'd been saving for the last year and kept hidden in an old coffee can near the woods. How long was it going to last? He had no idea how far eighty-eight dollars lasted in the city, but he was fairly sure it wouldn't be far enough. He was going to need to figure out a way to make some cash, quick.

Feeling panicked, he stopped to readjust his backpack.

"Simon? Hey! I thought that was you," Amelia Kinsinger called out, her voice ringing through the empty field like a bright, merry cowbell. "Whatcha doing?"

He froze. Then, attempting to gather himself, he turned to watch her trot closer. A bright smile was on her face. She looked really pleased to have spied him.

Though he knew better than to stay, he remained where he was. Even at only nine years old, little Amelia was the prettiest thing he'd ever seen. White-blond hair, crystal-blue eyes, and pale skin that never seemed to tan, she was everything delicate and perfect. She was also sheltered and his best friend's baby sister—and the only person who seemed to think he was worth something. Both of her brothers had confided that Amelia had a terrible crush on him. They'd thought it was embarrassing. Levi had even apologized for her.

He hadn't needed an apology, though. Simon had always thought Amelia's infatuation made him something special. He'd never let on that he noticed the way she always looked at him. He never acted annoyed when she rushed over to tell him about her day. Instead of making fun of her, he'd been patient and often sat with her when her older siblings were too busy.

But that said, he'd always taken care for her not to see him like this. He wanted to look worthy in her eyes. Not beaten and bruised.

"Can't talk right now, Amy," he bit out as he started forward.

He took care to keep his gaze fixated on the ground in front of him. Maybe then she wouldn't catch sight of his eye.

But, as usual, she didn't listen to his warning. Instead, she picked up her pace. "Did you know that the sun is almost set? Where you going? It's going to be dark soon."

"Ain't none of your business."

She stumbled, then caught herself before he reached out to steady her.

"Slow down, wouldja?" she said.

"Can't."

She sighed. "Why are ya being like this?" she asked, hurt in her tone. "All I asked is—"

"Simon! What happened to you?"

Unable to help himself, he drew to a stop. Then, because he probably was never going to see her again anyway, he allowed himself to lift his chin and let her look her fill. As he'd expected, she was staring at him in concern, her pale pink lips parted in wonder. And, he suspected, pity.

"Go on home, Amelia."

"Did you . . . did your *daed* do that?" she whispered, letting him know that his secret had never actually been one. "Do you need something? Do ya need some help? 'Cause my *daed*'s home. If we went to him, I bet he'd help ya."

That was why she meant so much to him. Here he was, bruised and battered, running away from home, and she thought he could still be saved. "Your *daed* can't help."

Tentatively, she held out a hand. Then, to his shock, she swiped at a patch of skin just to the side of his lip. When he flinched at her touch, she looked at him with sad eyes. "Sorry, but your lip is bleeding." She held up her finger to show the stain.

Seeing his blood on her hand was one of the worst things he'd ever experienced. It symbolized everything that was his life . . . and everything he didn't want it to be. Unable to help himself, he grabbed her hand and roughly swiped it on his shirt. "Wash your hands when you get home, hear me?"

"Oh. All right. But . . . but, Simon, won't you come with me? You could wash up, too."

"*Nee*. I've gotta go."

"You're leaving, aren't you?" she asked softly. "Just like your brother and sister did."

He couldn't lie to her. "*Jah*. I'm leaving. Just like Jeremy and Tess did."

"Please, don't."

As much as he would have liked to do anything she asked, he couldn't do that. "Listen, do me a favor, wouldja? Don't tell nobody you saw me."

Her bottom lip trembled. "But—"

"They'll find out soon enough. Just . . . just let me go, okay?" Then he did what he'd sworn he'd never do. He looked at her directly in the eyes and let her see his pain. "I have to do this, Amy."

Around a ragged sigh, looking so very sad, she nodded. "Okay."

"Bye, Amelia. You take care of yourself."

He started walking before she could reply. Before he did something stupid and followed her to her house. Before he thought about staying just a little longer so he could see her again.

He started walking because no matter how difficult and scary it was to leave, he knew for certain it was always going to be a whole lot worse at home.

Chapter 1

Thursday, October 1

P rincess, *nee!*" Amelia shouted as she scrambled down the front steps. "Stop!"

But Princess didn't hear her. Actually, that probably wasn't true. Princess no doubt heard her just fine. She simply didn't care to pay much attention to what Amelia wanted her to do.

Instead, the six-month-old pygmy goat continued to nonchalantly chew Oscar's leash.

From what Amelia could tell, the goat had been munching on it for some time. A good section of it was missing.

Thank heavens her sister Rebecca's bulldog puppy was unaware that he was free. Instead of running off as most dogs were wont to do, he was plopped on his side, enjoying the unexpected warmth of the October sun.

After picking up the pup—who, at twenty pounds, was now really too big to carry—and depositing him inside the screen door of the house, Amelia braced herself. It was time to convince Princess that she really, really needed to begin minding her new owner.

Her pet had a silky white coat, long eyelashes, and beady black eyes. Princess was pretty, smart, and could climb almost anything. She was also as ornery as one might expect of a young doe.

Everyone had warned Amelia about this. Her siblings had begged her to return Princess to the farm where she'd bought her, saying that none of them had time to properly train the animal. But Amelia had steadfastly ignored both the warnings and the entreaties. She'd wanted this goat. Actually, she had wanted something to call her own, and a goat would do.

It seemed she was as stubborn as her pet.

"You silly girl," Amelia said. "Rope ain't *gut* for you. You must learn to leave it alone."

Princess bleated in reply.

Unable to help herself, she laughed. "*Jah,* that is what I thought you might say." After carefully pulling the last bit of rope out of Princess's mouth, Amelia wrapped an arm around the pesky animal's neck and guided her to the barn. "Lucky for you, I just put some fresh alfalfa in your stall. You can get your fill of that while I do my chores."

Just as she was about to step inside her cozy stall, however, Princess balked. With a grunt and a bleat, she pulled away.

"Princess, I ain't got time for this. It's already two in the afternoon. I need to work on supper." And the garden. And sweep the floors. All the chores that were up to Amelia to complete since she was the lone member of her household still at home.

Really wishing that she'd put a harness or collar on her little goat, Amelia grabbed Princess around the middle and pulled her forward.

But the doe froze, looking panicked, and bleated loudly.

Frustrated beyond measure, Amelia pulled harder. "Come, now. I know you are stubborn, but you must start minding me!"

Princess curled her lips, revealing lots of shiny, white, sharp teeth.

Amelia glared right back. "What has gotten into you?" Stepping into the stall, she yanked on Princess again.

"Bleat!" Princess protested frantically, and then kicked out her back legs, then the front, just like a bucking bronco.

One tiny, surprisingly sharp hoof made contact with Amelia's shin.

More surprised than anything, Amelia threw her hands up in the air as she fell to the floor of the stall. And when her hand flew out to catch herself, she discovered why Princess had not wanted to be anywhere near her home.

Because Amelia's left hand landed on a snake.

It didn't take kindly to the interruption. It slithered, hissed, and bit her hand.

Amelia cried out.

Princess scrambled farther away.

Fighting pain in both her palm and leg, Amelia gathered her wits, hobbled out of the stall, and at last leaned back against the wooden enclosure. Then she did exactly what she'd tried so hard to never do . . .

She burst into tears. Terrible, loud, unapologetic tears. She was alone, she was in pain, and suddenly, she'd had enough. More than enough.

Amelia Kinsinger cried for her mother, who'd died when

Amelia was only seven. She cried for her father, who'd recently perished in a fire in her family's lumber mill. She cried for her brother Levi, who had left town soon after.

In short, she cried for everything she'd ever lost and everything she still had.

But most of all, she cried because there was currently no one around to hear.

IT SEEMED HE wasn't capable of staying away.

Yet, as Simon Hochstetler approached the stately white house that the Kinsingers had lived in for generations, he knew his best friend didn't want him calling on his little sister. And for most of his life he'd honored Lukas Kinsinger's wishes. But about four months ago, Simon had decided he was tired of waiting.

He was twenty-eight years old. Now he was a manager at Kinsinger Lumber and had over thirty men reporting to him. More importantly, he'd been in love with Amelia Kinsinger for years. Since his return to Charm two years ago, he'd kept his distance out of respect for both her age and the fact that she was his best friend's little sister, but when Amelia had started talking to him more, gazing at him longer, and smiling shyly whenever he teased her, Simon knew she returned his feelings. Since he was either going to hurt Amelia or disappoint Lukas, Simon knew there was only one way to go.

And because he was not the type of man to wait when he wanted something bad enough, Simon had since found a way to see Amelia: A few weeks ago he'd begun to see her on the sly, visiting her when he knew no one else would be around.

He wasn't proud of this.

If Amelia's parents had been alive, he would have done whatever it took to persuade them to accept him as a prospective suitor. But they had both gone up to Heaven and there was no way he was going to beg and plead his case to his childhood friend or Amelia's sister, Rebecca. Amelia was twenty-two and fully able to tell him if she didn't want him around. So far, she'd been delighted by his visits.

He'd told himself his visits were to give her some company— because Amelia worked at home by herself every day. But the truth was that Simon simply needed to be around her. Amelia was sweet, kind, and honest. She was beautiful, too. She was actually everything he'd ever wanted. More than he'd ever dared to yearn for.

Being in her company made him forget the mistakes he'd made. Her smiles gave him hope and her acceptance made him feel clean and worthy. There was no way he was ever going to give that up without a fight.

Still, even though he didn't mind doing whatever it took to see her, Simon knew that wasn't fair to Amelia. She deserved to have a man court her publicly. She deserved to see that Simon was willing to overcome any obstacle in order for her to be happy.

In fact, he was practicing different ways to convince Lukas of this when he arrived at the Kinsingers' house. Then, just as he began to walk up the front steps, he realized that something wasn't quite right. It was too quiet, everything unnaturally still. Usually, Amelia would be outside on the front porch with two Mason jars of iced tea or lemonade, waiting for him.

This was unexpected. They'd had plans. Just yesterday, he'd asked if she would be willing to spend an hour with him. She'd smiled and nodded.

But Amelia was nowhere in sight. Instead, the front door

was open. Only their ratty-looking screen door was preventing Oscar from getting out. The dog was staring at him in a pitiful way. He whined and pawed at the screen.

"Hey, boy," Simon murmured. "What's going on here?"

Oscar gazed up at him with sad eyes and whined some more.

Simon was growing more concerned by the minute.

"Amelia?" he called out.

She didn't answer.

Opening the screen door, he let Oscar waddle through, then followed him back down the steps. Immediately, Oscar did his business. Then, with a little grunt, he trotted toward the barn as quickly as his stocky legs could take him.

His heart in his throat, Simon followed on his heels.

"Amelia?" he called out again.

At last he heard a gasp, followed by a small cry.

He picked up his pace, dust flying up around his thick work boots. "Amelia, where are ya?"

"I'm . . . I'm in the barn."

Her voice didn't sound right. Running now, he followed the pup inside, then froze at the sight before him.

Amelia was sitting on the dirt floor of the barn crying. Her light pink dress was wrinkled and dusty. Her usually carefully pressed white *kapp* was smudged with dirt. Even in the dim light he could see that her cheeks were deathly pale, her nose and eyes were red from crying, and she was holding one hand awkwardly in the other.

He knelt by her side. "Amelia, what happened?" He didn't even bother with asking if she was all right. She so obviously wasn't.

She hiccupped. "There was a snake in Princess's stall." She waved her hand. "It—it bit my hand."

Simon was barely able to push aside his panic as he reached for her hand. Only the experiences of his past allowed him to control himself. "Are you sure? Was it a rattler? How long ago did this happen?"

"An hour ago. Maybe a little longer? And I'm not sure what kind it was," she said. Gazing at her hand that was now firmly held in his own, she visibly gathered herself. "It was a rat snake, I think. Nothing poisonous. At least, I'm fairly sure about that. But, Simon, it still hurts terribly."

Feeling marginally better, Simon forced his body to relax. If a copperhead or rattler had bit her, she would've likely been feeling much worse. She might have even passed out. But that didn't mean he didn't feel for her. Snake bites, venomous or not, were scary experiences.

"I reckon it does." Turning her hand, he searched for the puncture wounds. They were located at the bottom of her palm, less than an inch from her wrist. The affected area was slightly swollen and red. Most of the skin around it looked angry. Even if the snake hadn't been poisonous, Simon knew the bite should probably be checked out.

"Let's get you on the porch. Once you get settled, I'll hitch up Stormy to the buggy. We'll run over to the emergency clinic in Berlin."

When she looked up at him with a fierce expression, he braced himself for an argument. Amy was proud, and she hated being coddled. Furthermore, she seemed to be under the misconception that her needs weren't all that important.

Ever since Lukas had taken over the day-to-day operations at the mill following her father's death, she'd seemed intent on doing everything at home without complaint or help. And even though Rebecca, along with Lukas's new wife, Darla, helped for a few hours every now and then, it didn't make up for the fact that Amelia alone tended the animals, cared for the garden, cleaned the house, did the laundry, and cooked supper every single day.

But to Simon's surprise, instead of arguing, Amelia nodded.

Unable to help himself, he brushed her wet cheek with the side of his thumb. "I'm glad you understand," he said gently. "Now, give me your hand and I'll help you up."

But when she tried to move, she winced, then cried out.

He froze. "What's wrong?"

Averting her face, she started crying again—quiet, thick tears that cascaded down her cheeks and broke his heart.

Concerned, he crouched by her side and promptly forgot all his intentions of treating her in a calm albeit friendly way. Sidling closer, he wrapped an arm around her shoulders. "Amy, honey? Talk to me, *jah*?"

After taking a fortifying breath, she nodded. "Something else happened, Simon. Princess got scared of the snake and she kicked my shin. It hurts something awful. E-Even worse than my hand. I tried to get up, but I couldn't put any weight on it."

With effort, he refrained from reacting. The last thing she needed was for him to get upset about her injuries or say what was at the center of his mind—that he'd known it wasn't safe for her to be alone on the farm for hours at a time, day after day. But, of course, casting blame wouldn't help her feel better.

"Which leg did she kick?"

Awkwardly, she pointed to the one stretched out. "That one."

The hem of her dress was resting about mid-calf. He lifted

the fabric to her knee. Not seeing anything from that angle, he started to turn her calf when she cried out.

Growing alarmed, he moved to her other side so he could see the full extent of the injury. A large—very large—black-and-blue mark decorated her leg. It was extremely swollen and slightly misshapen.

He would bet money that the bone was broken. Visions of her sitting on the floor of the dusty barn in pain cut him deeply.

Once again, he ached to corner Lukas, Rebecca, and the missing Levi and give them a piece of his mind. Yes, Amelia was an adult, but she had been given no choice. While the three of them spent their days however they wanted to, Amelia was stuck at home alone. He'd told Lukas more than once that he worried something would happen to Amelia and she would be alone and helpless.

He wasn't exactly happy to have been proven right.

But none of that mattered now. All that mattered was taking care of Amelia and getting her help as soon as possible.

"Change of plans," he said as he pulled out his work cell phone. "We need to get you to the hospital."

The skin around her mouth whitened. "Do ya really think that is necessary?"

"I'm afraid so. I think your leg is broken."

After staring at him for a few seconds, she sighed. "I'm afraid it is, too," she whispered.

After pausing for a moment to give thanks that the bishop had allowed him to purchase a cell phone for work, he dialed 9-1-1. He'd deal with the consequences of using the phone for a nonwork-related reason at a later date.

He had to walk out the barn door to get a signal, but God was good. In no time at all, he'd been connected to the emergency operator, explained Amelia's situation, and relayed her address. Once he was assured they were on their way, he turned to her. "What do you want me to tell Lukas?"

"Don't call him yet."

"Amelia, I bet he could get here before the ambulance leaves. Besides, he ain't going to be happy to be kept in the dark."

She shook her head again. "*Nee.* If you call the mill, it's going to send Luke and Rebecca into a dither. They'll run home and take charge." Sounding weary, she said, "I'm not ready for that right now."

Everything inside of him disagreed with her. "They love you, Amelia. You keeping them away ain't right."

"I know. But can't you contact them after we get to the hospital? That's not too long to wait."

Though he still didn't feel right about it, he didn't argue. She was in pain and she was also his weakness. He hated to refuse her anything. "The ambulance will be here soon. What do you need from the house?"

Relief filled her blue eyes. "*Danke,* Simon. All I need is my purse. It's on the kitchen counter."

"I'll be right back. You sit tight." Then he went to put a pouting Princess in one of the empty horse stalls and guided Oscar back to the house.

Inside, unable to help himself, Simon wrote Lukas and Rebecca a brief note. He'd just finished it when he heard the sirens.

After grabbing her purse, he rushed back to her side. When she gazed up at him, her pretty eyes shining with unshed tears, he attempted to smile. "The ambulance is almost here. They'll take you to the hospital and give you something for your pain."

She still looked agitated. "Simon, I'm afraid," she admitted. Looking ashamed, she whispered, "The hospital brings back many bad memories."

"I know it does." He'd been seated by her side both times she'd discovered one of her parents had died. That hospital waiting room, with its worn carpet floor, vinyl chairs, and faint bleachy smell would always trigger bad memories.

"Would you go with me?"

"Of course. I'm not going to leave your side, Amelia. You couldn't get rid of me if you tried."

Her bottom lip trembled as she attempted to smile. *"Danke."*

"Never thank me for something like this. I don't want to be anywhere else."

She smiled as she pushed back some stray strands of her white-blond hair. Only Amelia could look beautiful at a time like this.

He smiled at her again before walking out the barn door and waving to the approaching ambulance.

"She's in here!" he called out when a man and woman opened the doors to the vehicle.

As he watched them get out a stretcher, Simon realized that he had now made his choice regarding Amelia. He was done thinking of other people. He was done biding his time.

"Are you a relative?" the man asked.

"Boyfriend," he replied, not caring that it wasn't technically the truth.

As far as he was concerned, she would be his girl soon enough.

Chapter 2

Most of the time, Lukas Kinsinger was able to take his many responsibilities in stride. He liked being the oldest and he liked being needed.

Usually, he was the first one awake in the house. While it was still dark outside, he quietly got up and got dressed, taking care not to disturb Darla. Then he went out to the barn. There, he fed their three horses and two dairy cows, gave Princess some attention and made sure she had fresh water. Then, while the animals were contentedly eating, he would head back to the house just as the sun was peeking over the edge of the horizon.

While the coffee finished brewing, he would organize his papers and pack his lunch for work. Finally, he would creep upstairs to kiss his wife goodbye just as her alarm clock went off.

By then, his sister Amelia would have made him a breakfast sandwich. He'd take it with him and eat while he walked the short distance to work.

By the time he walked through the front door of Kinsinger Lumber every morning, he was more than ready to face the myriad of responsibilities that awaited him as the head of the lumber mill. He worked hard, he solved problems, he kept his cool, and he didn't stop.

Several times a week he headed home as close to five o'clock as possible. This was for the sole purpose of helping his little sister, Amelia.

And that was how he always thought of her: little. She might be twenty-two. She might run their household and be extremely capable in a number of ways, but in his mind, she was still the adorable nine-year-old with white-blond hair, earnest blue eyes, and a heart and soul that was sweeter than most anyone he knew.

The fact was that he adored Amelia. She was special to him and had always been that way.

He hated the fact that she currently spent the majority of each day alone at their farm, caring for their animals and garden and home and life without a word of complaint. So, even though Rebecca still stopped by often, and Darla was around a lot, too, he tried to spend time with her each day.

He didn't care that she'd never asked him to do that. It didn't matter that there was usually little to do besides keep Amelia company while she cooked supper.

No matter what, she would always be his little sister.

But the moment he strode into the barn, it was obvious something was wrong. Stormy looked agitated and Princess was bleating mournfully. She wasn't even in the right stall. A lump formed in his throat as panic overtook him—that same feeling of panic that had engulfed him months earlier when he'd real-ized the back warehouse of the lumber mill was on fire and not everyone had gotten out.

Now, fearing the worst, he rushed to the house. It was in disarray. Two of the cupboards were open, dishes were in the sink, jars of soup and half an onion rested on the counter.

And then he saw the note.

Lukas was so horrified, he had to read it several times for the full meaning to register. Amelia had been both bitten by a snake and kicked by her goat. She'd sat by herself for over an hour, injured and in pain. Helpless.

Until Simon had arrived.

Then she'd been rushed by ambulance to the hospital—all while Lukas had been worrying about shipments from Michigan and needy customers in Columbus.

Simon had found his little sister. Simon had been the person to take care of her and see to her needs. Not Rebecca. Not him.

Pulling out his work cell phone, he contacted Jeff, one of his English managers at the mill. Luckily, he answered on the first ring.

"Hey, Lukas," Jeff said. "Are you calling about the Emerson account? Because if you are, I gotta—"

"It's not that," he interrupted. "It's . . ." Gathering himself, he blurted, "Jeff, I need a favor."

"Name it," Jeff replied immediately, making Lukas realize he probably sounded as panicked as he felt.

"Amelia's been hurt and is on her way to the hospital. I need you to go tell Rebecca, then drive her here and pick me up, too. We've got to get to the hospital as soon as possible."

"Of course. Is . . . is Amelia okay?"

"I don't know," he said slowly. Though the question had been innocent enough, hearing it hurt. He forced himself to continue. "I don't know anything." Except for what he had read in Simon's blasted note.

"I'm walking to the front reception area right now. Expect me there in fifteen minutes, tops."

"Danke." Thinking of Rebecca's new husband, he blurted, "Oh, you better go tell Jacob Yoder, too. Rebecca's going to need him."

"Of course. I'll be there as soon as possible."

Lukas clicked off his phone and stared at the note again. There was no doubt that Rebecca was going to have a lot to say about Simon's visit. She had been fairly vocal about the fact that she didn't want Simon to court Amelia.

Lukas had agreed. On principle, at least. Amelia was special and sweet and innocent. His best friend in the world was none of those things. Actually, he was more jaded and world-weary than most Englishers. He'd had a difficult *rumspringa,* much of which he refused to talk about.

However, there was no way Simon could escape his history. After he left home at fifteen, he'd engaged in all sorts of illegal activities. Several years later, his poor choices caught up with him. He was with some men who stole a car. When they were arrested, Simon had been high on some kind of drugs.

He'd been sentenced to eighteen months in jail and served nine months of it. When he'd gotten out, he'd worked a number of odd jobs and struggled. Those struggles had eventually driven him to contact Lukas's *daed.*

From what Lukas had heard, his father had invited Simon to come to his office. They'd talked for hours. His father had even offered Simon a job at the mill. Lukas was also fairly sure that his father had given him money so he could get a place to live, too.

Neither his father nor Simon had ever talked about that.

As the months passed, Lukas's best friend had slowly returned to him. Simon was hardworking and punctual. Slowly, he started smiling again. Sometimes he joked.

But he never, ever, talked about his time on the streets or his months in a prison cell.

As Simon's best friend, Lukas had honored that request. Men needed to have their privacy, and everyone made their fair share of mistakes. Lukas knew Simon Hochstetler was a good man. An honorable one.

But a beau for Amelia? Lukas didn't think so. His sister had already been through way too much to be saddled with a man with a disreputable past. She deserved someone without a mass of skeletons in his closet.

As he rushed around the house, then out to the barn to check on the animals before Jeff arrived, Lukas tried not to imagine the worst. Amelia had been kicked by a goat and bitten by a snake. Those were bad things, but not necessarily life-threatening. He wasn't going back to the hospital to wait for someone to die again. Amelia was going to be just fine.

The Lord couldn't take one more person away from him.

He would never be so cruel.

THE STAFF AT the hospital couldn't have been nicer to Amelia. Someone had even brought her a glass of cranberry juice and a small bowl of orange sherbet. But that didn't mean Amelia wanted to sit in an uncomfortable hospital bed for even one more minute.

"Simon, can't you get me out of here?" Amelia pleaded. "This is an awful place." She hated hospitals. Hated them with every fiber of her being. The smell, the faint sounds, the feel of the scratchy cotton sheets—all of it made her skin crawl.

Simon was sitting in a vinyl chair next to her, his elbows resting on his knees. He had been watching her with a combination of amusement and concern on his face for the last two hours.

From the time the ambulance pulled onto her property with sirens blaring and lights flashing, he was true to his word. Unless Amelia was getting tests or X-rays, Simon stayed close to her side.

His lips quirked, as if he was trying to fend off a smile. "You know I'd help you if I could. But I can't, Amelia. The doctors said that you need to be observed until tomorrow morning."

"But that means that I'll be poked and prodded all night long."

Of course, that wasn't what she really cared about. She wasn't afraid of needles and didn't really care if nurses came to check on her regularly. But being in the hospital until sometime tomorrow? Every memory and fear that she'd carefully tamped down was bubbling to the surface and threatening to ruin the last of her remaining composure.

"I'm afraid so. But you'll be all right," he said with complete confidence.

Embarrassed that she had sounded so ungrateful and childish, she nodded. "*Jah*. You are right. I will be just fine." No matter how painful the memories were, it was time to stop complaining and fretting. "*Danke* for taking care of me and for staying by my side. If you would like to leave now, you can go ahead."

He smiled. "I would *not* like that."

"I'll be all right. You said you called Lukas."

"By the time I called, Mercy was manning the reception desk. She told me that Lukas had already read the note I left and had called someone to pick him and Rebecca up. They'll be here any minute, I reckon."

That's what she was afraid of. She didn't want to repay Simon's kindness by subjecting him to a bunch of questions from Rebecca and Lukas. "If they're on their way, I'll be fine."

"I'm not leaving you alone, Amy."

His words were so firm, so sure, she melted. For most of her life, she'd loved Simon. It wasn't a crush; it was meaningful and true. Steadfast. Even better, she was pretty sure Simon felt the same way, especially since she'd heard him tell the ambulance workers that he was her boyfriend. She knew that they were meant to be together. And maybe one day they would be.

If her siblings would ever allow such a thing.

Now Amelia just had to remind everyone that she was tougher than they realized. She would survive this episode just like she'd survived everything else in life.

"Are you in much pain?"

She pointed to the IV in her hand. "Not so much. They've been putting some pain medicine in it."

Staring at her leg, Simon frowned. "I fear you are going to hurt worse pretty soon. It was a pretty good break."

"*Jah*. Have I told you how glad I am that you found me?"

A shadow filled his gaze. "I am glad I was there, too. I don't know what I would have done if you had been sitting there for longer than you already were."

She giggled softly. "What *you* would have done?"

He leaned back and propped one foot on his opposite knee. "Of course! We need to talk about how *I* would be dealing with *your* injury," he teased. "This crisis is all about me. Ain't so?"

She sighed dramatically. "Of course, Simon." What he didn't realize was that he *was* all she wanted to think about. He was so handsome with his light-brown hair, stark cheekbones, and hazel eyes. He even looked slightly dangerous. It was disconcerting and appealing, all at the same time.

"Seriously, I'm going to stay as long as I can, but the nurse has already let me know that I shouldn't have been here in the first place."

"I don't know about that." After a pause, she added, "Family and boyfriends can visit, *jah*?"

"Uh-oh. You heard that?"

She noticed he didn't look especially embarrassed. "I couldn't help but hear it, you were pretty loud. And adamant."

He looked down at his knees. "I'm sorry. But I was prepared to say anything that would allow me to stay by your side. At least until Lukas or Rebecca came."

It sounded as if he was forcing himself to say the last part, almost like he would prefer to have her to himself for as long as possible. And because he was being so honest, she decided to be honest, too. "I don't want them here."

"They're going to be upset that I didn't call them the minute I found you."

"You would have, but I asked you not to."

For the first time, he looked unsure. "I bowed to your wishes, but I don't think that was the right thing to do."

"It was. The minute they arrive, they're going to overreact and badger me with questions that I don't want to answer."

His hazel eyes gleamed, silently signaling his agreement. "Don't be unkind. You know they love you."

"I love them. But that doesn't mean I want them to make a difficult situation even worse."

"Don't worry. I won't let them misbehave or upset you."

"Simon, your words are sweet, but we're talking about Lukas

and Rebecca here. They're going to say what's on their minds. And loudly, too."

He shook his head. "Not this time."

Usually, Amelia would simply leave a statement like that alone. Simon sounded so sure. Adamant. However, she also knew her brother and sister. "How do you intend to keep them in line?"

"Don't you worry about that. All you need to do is rest and be assured that I won't let them cause a scene or bully you. I've had enough of them treating you as if you are a little girl."

"Simon—"

Her door flew open as Rebecca, Lukas, Darla, and Jacob charged in. They sounded like a herd of cattle, talking too loudly, rushing to her side as they exclaimed over her cast and the bandage on her hand.

Amelia braced herself. Then blinked when she realized that Simon had gotten to his feet and was standing next to her.

"That's enough, everyone," he said calmly. "All of you need to settle down. Now."

Just like that, the whole room turned silent as her siblings and their spouses each turned to stare at Simon. Tension filled the air.

Chapter 3

Ignoring Simon, Lukas studied Amelia carefully. "I got here as soon as I heard. What in the world did you do?"

What had *she* done? That was the first thing he had to say? She blinked. Though she knew he wasn't being insensitive on purpose, his words hurt. Suddenly, she felt like she was a young girl again. A young, pesky little sister who needed constant supervision and constant bailing out. Looking from Lukas to the rest of her family, her mouth went dry.

Simon cleared his throat. "You aren't helping things, Lukas. Calm yourself, *jah*?"

For the first time, Lukas looked directly at Simon. "I'm as calm as I care to be right now. Why don't you step aside so I can talk to my sister?"

Just as Simon was about to shake his head, Amelia spoke. "It's all right, Simon. I need to do this." This was exactly the kind of scene that she'd hoped to avoid.

He leaned closer, warmth and worry in his expression. "You sure?"

"*Jah*."

Gritting his teeth, Simon moved across the room. Though she

missed his presence already, Amelia faced her family by herself. They loved her and cared about her. She simply needed to stand up to them for once.

"What happened?" Lukas asked.

She waved a hand across her body. "I think it's fairly obvious. I've got a broken leg and a sore hand."

Lukas's lips didn't even twitch. "I need you to be serious right now."

"I know. Well, you see, it all started when Princess didn't want to listen. Then, when I attempted to put her away, there was a snake in Princess's stall."

"A snake."

"*Jah.* It seems one was hiding in the straw. When I was trying to get Princess into her stall, she pulled out of my grip and kicked me. Next thing I knew, I fell on top of a snake, which then bit me."

"That goat broke your leg," Lukas said.

"Well, *jah.*"

"We need to get rid of that goat," Rebecca said, moving to stand by their brother. "She's been nothing but trouble."

Amelia was starting to hate that she was lying down while her siblings were standing over her. "*Nee,* that ain't true."

"We'll talk about it later, Amy," Lukas said. "Now I'm going to go find someone to tell me how you are really doing."

Amelia's bottom lip trembled in frustration. "Lukas, *I* know how I'm doing."

But he wasn't listening to her. Turning away, he started ordering everyone around. "Becky, you and Darla stay here with her. Jacob and I will—"

"That is enough," Simon said firmly. Though he stood against the window, his presence was still very apparent. Now his voice was so strong and forceful, Amelia was certain that the patients in the room next door had heard him.

Looking increasingly impatient, Lukas said, "Simon, *danke* for looking after my sister, but I've got it now. You can leave."

"*Nee,*" she whispered.

But she shouldn't have worried.

"I don't think so," Simon replied as he walked back to her side. Looking every bit the protector, he glared at her whole family. "For such a close-knit group, you all are fairly disappointing."

Darla raised her brows. "What?"

"Don't you think it's time you stopped treating Amelia like a wayward child?" Simon asked impatiently. "Not a one of you has even given her a hug or told her that you were worried about her. Why?" Raising his voice, he added, "Why are you all so determined to control the situation while ignoring what is really important?"

Rebecca blinked. "Are you really standing in my sister's hospital room lecturing us?"

Simon crossed his arms over his chest. "What does it look like?"

Ack! This was going from bad to worse. "I'll be all right, Simon," she whispered. "You don't have to intervene."

"*Nee.* I'm pretty sure I do." Looking around her room, his expression turned even more intent. "Someone in here needs to put your needs first."

"Simon, you are right," Rebecca said after a small pause. "We have been behaving pretty poorly." Turning to Amelia, she looked contrite. "I'm sorry."

Though it was good to hear the apology, Amelia couldn't forget that it had been brought on by Simon's interference. She was so, so tired of her well-meaning siblings ignoring her wishes. "Rebecca, I'm glad you apologized, but that ain't the problem. You all came in here and started taking charge like I can't speak for myself. I don't like you all managing me. Stop it."

Hurt showed in Rebecca's eyes. "You know we're simply trying to help you."

"*Jah*. But how would you feel if our situations were reversed?"

When Rebecca opened her mouth, then closed it in confusion, Jacob chuckled softly. "I think she's got a point there."

A nurse came in. "Ah, Amelia, look at you," she quipped in a bright voice. "You now have both your boyfriend and your family here. You are the most popular girl in town."

Lukas stiffened. "Boyfriend?"

Oblivious to the new tension in the room, the nurse grinned. Practically gushing, she said, "Oh, yes. The whole nurses' station has been talking about how wonderful he is."

"Simon?" Rebecca asked.

The nurse smiled at Simon. "I've never seen a more devoted man." Turning to Amelia, she winked. "We're all jealous, Amelia. He's handsome as all get-out and doesn't want to leave your side. He's a keeper, for sure."

As she picked up Amelia's wrist and took her pulse, Amelia felt her cheeks get hot. Her siblings and their spouses stared at each other in stunned silence.

And Simon? Well, he simply folded his arms over his chest and grinned before the nurse politely asked them all to give Amelia some privacy.

THE MOMENT THE nurse gave them permission, Lukas, Jacob, and Rebecca rushed back into Amelia's room. Simon followed on their heels. He not only wasn't in any hurry to leave Amelia's side, he didn't trust Lukas and Rebecca to hold their tongues.

"I think we should talk about this," Rebecca said the moment she got to Amelia's side. "You and Simon courting on the sly ain't good."

Amelia raised an eyebrow. "What are you wanting to do, Becky? Ground me?"

Simon had to bite back a smile as Rebecca exchanged a puzzled look with Lukas. It seemed Amelia was finally tired of her brother and sister treating her like she was a recalcitrant teenager.

"That ain't fair, Amy," Rebecca said. "You know I'm concerned because I care about you."

"I care about you both, and that is the reason I'm not yelling at you for acting like I'm a naughty child," Amelia said wearily. "But I will if you push this."

Looking troubled, Lukas said, "Maybe we should let Amy get some rest."

"*Jah,* I think that's a good idea. Actually, you might even want to head home," Amelia said. "I'm tired."

Though she sounded sincere, Simon suspected she didn't really feel that way. After all, before they'd arrived, she'd been telling Simon how much she hated being in the hospital. Here she was again, trying to take care of everyone from her hospital bed in the same way she did at home. Amelia excelled at helping others, often at her own expense.

"We'll see ya later, Amy," Rebecca said softly. "I am glad you're going to be all right."

"*Danke.*"

"Come on, guys," Rebecca said as she walked to the door. "Let's let her rest."

"Simon, would you stay with me?"

Before he could reply, Lukas shook his head. "Simon and I have some things we need to discuss. Now's as good a time as any."

Twin spots of color appeared on her cheeks. "Lukas."

Simon's temper began to burn. Yet again Lukas was trying to make everything right instead of realizing just how wrong his interference actually was.

But Lukas was as stubborn as his sweet sister. Knowing that, Simon stood up. "He's right."

Amelia frowned. "*Nee,* Simon."

He hated that she was trying to look after him even when she was sitting in a hospital bed. "It's okay," he said gently as he leaned close. "We need to clear the air. It might as well be now." Ignoring Lukas's glower, Simon leaned closer to Amelia. "Did you forget that I said that I was going to take care of everything? I will."

Still pointedly ignoring her brother, she shook her head. "But there's nothing to take care of."

"I'm afraid I don't agree. Your brother isn't going to give either of us a moment's peace until he has his say."

"Don't let him browbeat you," Amelia cautioned.

"I won't. Try not to worry, okay? Why don't you rest for a few minutes? You could probably use a few minutes of peace and quiet."

"But you'll come back?"

"Of course I will." Turning to Lukas, he said, "Let's go out in the hall."

The moment Amelia's door was shut behind them, Lukas folded his arms across his chest. "Where do you want to do this?"

Though Simon would rather not have their much-needed conversation in the middle of the hospital, someone needed to put Lukas in his place. Because Levi was nowhere to be found, it looked like he was getting the job.

"Since you're in such a hurry," he said, "how about right here? I have nothing to hide."

"Absolutely not," said Lukas. "I want to talk to you without half the hospital listening."

"Fine. Let's go outside, then. "There's a picnic area. We have less chance of being interrupted or observed there."

Lukas started walking toward the elevators. "That'll do."

Neither of them said a word as the elevator dinged, the doors opened, and they descended three floors. Together, they walked silently down the hallway, out a side door, and along a covered walkway until they were standing in front of a freshly painted wooden picnic table.

Simon sat down on one of the benches while Lukas perched on the tabletop of another nearby.

Though he was feeling more than a little uneasy, Simon was good at pretending otherwise. He did that, leaning back and stretching his legs out in front of him. "What did you want to discuss?"

Lukas rolled his eyes. "Don't play innocent with me. You know I ain't happy about your interest in my sister."

"Yeah, you've made your feelings well known." He didn't even attempt to hide his sarcasm.

"Since you know how I feel, why have you ignored my wishes?"

"Because I'm not interested in courting *you*, Lukas. What's happening between Amelia and me is between the two of us.

Not you. And not Rebecca," he added, just in case Lukas was of the mind to bring her up, too.

"I'm head of the household."

Simon brushed off the statement. "Amelia is old enough to make up her own mind. You know she is."

"She is," Lukas agreed after a pause.

"If you agree, then why are you being so difficult?" Unable to keep the derision from his voice, he added, "It makes no sense. You are acting as if I'm an Englisher stranger up to no good."

"Hardly that."

"It would ease your sister's mind if you would stop this foolishness and give us your blessing."

Looking increasingly uncomfortable, Lukas said, "You know I cannot."

Tired of going round and round, Simon got to the heart of the matter. "You know that I would never hurt her. You know my intentions are honorable. Honestly, Lukas, what is the problem?"

"The problem is that Amelia doesn't know everything about you. She doesn't know what you did."

Unease made his teeth clench. "What I did?"

"During your *rumspringa,* Simon." Lukas closed his eyes, then pulled off his hat, slapped it on the picnic table, and ran a hand through his hair. "You're my best friend. I know you're a good man. One of the best."

Simon shifted uneasily. "But?"

"But you are not the right person for my sweet and innocent sister."

"I was baptized. I joined the church. Everything that you're referring to is behind me now. You know that."

"How can it ever be? You have marks to prove what you did. Those can never be erased."

"Those marks are tattoos, Lukas. Simple tattoos. Not marks of the devil."

"She will be shocked when she sees them."

"I think Amelia will be surprised, not shocked. And even if she is, she'll get used to them."

Lukas slapped his hat back on his head. "We both know I'm not talking just about a couple of tattoos." He stared at him meaningfully.

Which, of course, drove Simon crazy. "Why don't you just say it?" he taunted.

"You got those tattoos in prison. In *prison,* Simon."

Even after all this time, the reminder hurt as badly as his father's cane used to. "Not all of them. Only the first."

Lukas ground his teeth. "Are you truly going to brush off your time in prison, too?"

Simon actually wished he could delete it from his memory. "I was in prison for nine months for participating in a carjacking," he said succinctly. "At the time, I didn't even know the men I was with were doing such things. I thought they were only buying drugs."

"*Only buying drugs.* Do you hear yourself?"

"Oh, *jah.* I do, for sure. And I remember everything from that time. How lost I was. What a fog I was in. How that prison smelled. How I regretted my actions, but I had no choice but to pay the price." Lowering his voice, he added, "I accepted my punishment like a man. I did my time and I went directly to the bishop and pleaded with him to let me atone for my transgressions. And I have, Lukas. I have admitted my sins, asked for forgiveness, and have since vowed to live a life that I'm proud of."

After his lengthy speech, Simon stared at his best friend. He'd never been so forthcoming about his past with Lukas. He'd never wanted Lukas to look at him with disdain, the way he was now.

"You see?" Lukas said. "This is what I'm talking about. You've never told me about any of this before."

"There was no need. It's in the past."

"*Nee,* I don't think it is. As far as I can tell, you've never actually dealt with it. All you've done is pretend that it didn't happen. But you can't erase the past. The memories linger."

"I know that."

Memories that he tried so hard to keep buried came to the surface. But the ones that he cringed at weren't of his teenaged years. No, they were from his childhood at his parents' house. Even now, he couldn't bring himself to think of it as his "home."

"I am a different man than I was." He clenched his right hand, hating how his voice now sounded hoarse.

"I think you are. But you are expecting Amelia to bear your burden and that ain't fair." Still barely looking at him, Lukas continued. "I never faulted you for rebelling. I understood why your brother and sister left the faith. I would have understood if you had done so, too. The things your parents did to you, Jeremy, and Tess—all in the name of the Lord? Well, it was terrible, indeed."

"Yet you are determined to hold it against me."

"*Nee.* I am your friend. I will always be your friend. Even if my father hadn't hired you, I would have. I have been blessed to know you."

"If you really mean all that, why are you standing in my way?"

Lukas sighed. "Because we are not talking about you and me. We're talking about Amelia, who has already lost so much."

"I don't want to *take* anything from her, Luke."

"You want to take her innocence. If she marries you, she's going to have to learn about the things you've done. She's going to learn things about places she should never know about and people that she shouldn't realize exist."

"She is a grown woman, not a sheltered child. But even with that said, I have no intention of sharing with her all the things I've done. She doesn't need to know."

"If she becomes your wife, she'll have that right, don't you think?" Lukas asked softly.

"I will promise to honor and cherish her. Not taint her with my past."

"But our pasts make up who we are," Lukas said. "Look. I promised myself that I'd always protect her. I owe it to my parents' memory to do that. In some ways, she's the best of our family. She's tender and sweet. I want her to find a man who will honor that and keep her that way. Not ruin all her illusions. As much as I love you like a brother . . . you are not good enough for her."

He was not enough. He was never going to be enough.

Even though he knew everything Lukas said was true, the words hurt so much that Simon could barely talk. He settled for nodding.

True regret filled Lukas's gaze, reminding Simon that before his infatuation with Amelia, he'd had a strong friend in Lukas. "I'm sorry, Simon. I really am. However, with my parents gone, I have to put my sister's needs first. Someone has to do the job our parents would've if they had been here."

"I understand," he replied. And unfortunately, he did. "Of course you need to put her needs above all else."

"She needs someone without a past. Someone who won't saddle her with more hurt and pain."

Simon nodded. Then, finding the strength from somewhere deep inside of himself, he said, "I need to get out of here. I know I said I'd be right back, but tell her . . . tell her that something came up at work. I'll stop by tomorrow."

"I'm not sure that is a good idea."

"It might not be. But there is no way I am going to break things off without an explanation. I'll do what you want. But I am coming back tomorrow to see her."

"All right." Looking weary, Lukas stood up. "Thank you for understanding."

He was willing to give up everything he wanted and give Lukas his due, but he didn't understand. At least, his heart didn't.

Simon was barely able to nod before turning away and walking through the wrought-iron gate toward the hospital parking lot. After he heard the door close and he knew Lukas was out of view, he closed his eyes and exhaled.

Simon tried to tell himself that he should be glad he was doing the right thing. That he was going to be glad when Amelia found a better man whose skin wasn't marked by scars and ink.

But all he could feel was the bitter pain of loss. His body felt cold. Empty.

As cold and empty as he'd felt when he'd been locked in that cellar, surrounded by jars of food. And forbidden to touch a one.

Lost in thought, he almost didn't hear his name being called.

"Simon, is that you?"

When he turned around, he felt as if he'd just slammed into a brick wall. Standing right there in the middle of the parking lot was Tess.

His sister, whom he hadn't seen in over a decade.

Chapter 4

Tess felt like she wasn't getting enough air in her lungs.

She'd called out Simon's name on impulse. Almost as if her heart had known her little brother was near before her mind could fully comprehend it. Standing next to the main entrance, staring at her like she was a stranger, was her brother. Who she hadn't seen in fifteen years.

As she stood staring back at him, time seemed to stand still. Once again, she was sitting in a public park weeks after she'd run away, feeling as if she was completely alone in the world.

For the most part, she was.

After running away from home when she was fifteen, she'd endured three terrible months of living on the streets. Her older brother, Jeremy, who had run away before her, had gotten mixed up in a bad crowd. It only took one night with him and his friends for her to know that a second night in their company was a recipe for disaster. So, she'd left. Soon, she'd found refuge in public libraries and parks. She kept what little money she had hidden and talked to no one . . . until she met Jill, a police officer who became her foster mother and saved her life.

But now, for the first time in fifteen years, she was in Amish country. And, just after shaking hands with a pair of doctors at the Millersburg Hospital, she'd turned to go to her car and walked right into the last person she ever thought she'd see.

"Simon?" she called out again. This time a tremor in her voice betrayed her nervousness.

He blinked those hazel eyes—an exact match to her own—and stared hard at her. At her shoulder-length hair that she'd paid a fortune to put golden highlights in. At her slim-fitting black suit. Her pumps with a designer insignia imprinted on the heel. Tess stood silently, knowing that she looked so very different from the scared, beaten Amish girl she'd once been.

The girl who'd left one night without telling him goodbye. Who'd never contacted him, even when she'd heard that he had gotten arrested and was in jail.

Then, at last, Simon's gaze settled on the faint scar that marred her bottom lip. He exhaled. "Tess," he said after a moment. "You're back."

She nodded, because she almost answered him in Pennsylvania Dutch. And because she was tempted to clarify his words. She wasn't really *back,* only there for work. But most of all, she held her tongue because she was about to either hug him or burst into tears. She'd pushed so many memories away, but she'd never wanted to forget her little brother.

Only the many ways she'd failed him.

"What are you doing here?"

The right answer, of course, was to tell him that she'd been at the hospital for work. The truth was that she'd never imagined she'd see him again. She'd never imagined that he'd ever want to see her again. After all, she'd left when he'd needed her. Then, after surviving another three years at home, he'd gone out into the world and made enough poor choices to earn himself a prison sentence. Though it made no sense, she'd always felt more than a little responsible for that.

She'd asked her foster mother to let her know when he'd been released from prison. Jill had done that, but she hadn't known what happened to him next. Tess had imagined Simon doing a great many things, but she'd never dreamed he'd return to Charm.

She certainly had never thought he'd still be Amish.

And because of all that, she'd assumed he was lost to her forever.

But that seemed too harsh. And, perhaps, not quite true. Maybe, in time, she would have felt brave enough to track him down.

"I don't know," she said at last with a shrug. "Simon, it's *gut* to see ya."

"Is it?"

She couldn't read his expression. Couldn't tell whether he was disappointed to see her, still angry with her for leaving, or simply didn't care. She wouldn't blame him for any of it. "Of course it is. I've missed you."

"It's been a long time."

It didn't escape her notice that he didn't echo her sentiment. "Do you ever see Jeremy?" she asked. "I heard he lives somewhere in northern Ohio now."

"Nee."

"And . . . our parents?" She couldn't call either of them mom or dad. Jill had become her mother.

"Never."

The statement—and the vehemence behind it—surprised her. "But you are still Amish."

He stared at her, looking down slightly. Making her realize that he wasn't the scared, skinny boy she'd abandoned. Instead, he was a good five inches taller than her, and probably had sixty or seventy pounds on her, too. He looked strong and fit and stalwart. She doubted anyone ever messed with him these days.

"I believe in God, Tess. I know He is a good and faithful God. I believe in our faith, too. I've never wanted to leave," he said quietly. "But that don't mean I believe in our parents. I left their *haus* as soon as I could. Just like you and Jeremy did."

Though they both knew why she'd left, she still felt guilty. "Do you hate me?"

"For leaving me? Of course not."

He'd said *leaving me*. Not *leaving*. That mattered.

"Sure?" She didn't know why she needed that reassurance, but she did.

He shrugged. "It doesn't do much good to regret our pasts. Ain't so? What's done is done."

He was right. The knowledge didn't make her feel better, but he was right. Suddenly, she knew that she couldn't leave him without trying to bridge their gap. "Hey, Simon, um, what are you doing now? Would you like to grab something to eat?" She attempted to smile, though her lips were quivering. "My treat."

He looked away from her. Sighed. Then nodded. "*Jah*. But you're not paying for my meal."

"Does that mean you're paying for mine?" she teased before she realized that once again her mouth had gotten the best of her.

"*Nee*." He started walking. "But I might next time," he said around a half-smile.

Tears filled her eyes as she swallowed hard in a futile attempt to remove the lump from her throat. Maybe he didn't hate her. Maybe somehow, some way, they could finally have a relationship like other brothers and sisters had.

Maybe it was time.

It seemed that Simon was exactly right. God was good. Tess had learned that truth years ago when Jill, a cop in a baseball cap, had picked her up and taken her home.

And she was now reminded of it when she looked at her brother. Who had somehow survived without any help from his older sister.

Tess didn't know if she could ever make amends, but she figured it was time to try.

Chapter 5

Rebecca and Darla were wonderful-*gut* women. The best. But Amelia wished they'd leave her alone.

Simon hadn't kept his promise after all. Thirty minutes after Lukas had practically dragged Simon out of the room, her brother returned by himself. Looking awkward and more than a little distant, he'd bid her a rather hasty goodbye. When she'd asked where Simon was, Lukas had told her a story about Simon needing to take care of some emergency at work.

A couple of hours after that, her sister and sister-in-law had returned to her bedside. Rebecca said she and Darla had thought it would be fun to enjoy some girl-time together.

But Amelia was definitely not having fun.

Her hand hurt, her leg was sore, and she was uncomfortable sitting in an unfamiliar room in a sterile hospital. The doctors and nurses were kind enough, but their care couldn't make up for the fact that she was far from home.

She also really, really wished that they would turn off the television. Rebecca had turned it on when Amelia hadn't been much of a conversationalist. She loved the remote control and flipped it incessantly. Then, to Amelia's dismay, she'd stopped on some kind of home shopping network.

And there it stayed.

Darla, in particular, was gazing at the screen in rapt attention. At the moment, the television hosts were showing gold and silver rings and talking about how everyone needed not one but two or three of them.

"I like the one with the purple birthstone the best," Darla declared as she playfully held out one slim hand like one of the models. "What do you think, Amelia?"

Another time, Amelia might have played along. Now all she wanted to do was sit quietly and try to figure out what was going on with Simon. "I have no need for any rings. Neither do you."

"Oh, I know that." Eyes shining, Darla held up her hand again. "Now stop being so serious and play along. What color is your birthstone?"

"I don't know."

"Look at the screen," Rebecca said helpfully. "It has the chart right there. I've got sapphires. That's the blue stone."

Amelia shrugged. "I've got an August birthday."

"That's peridot," Rebecca announced.

In spite of herself, Amelia studied the chart on the screen. "What is peridot?"

"I don't know, but it's green." Darla glanced at Amelia, then tilted her head. "I think it might look good on you. Not as good as sapphire, though. A girl with your blue eyes needs a blue ring."

Oh, brother.

"Maybe she could lie," Rebecca said. "We could both get sapphire birthstones."

"Maybe we could turn it off," Amelia said peevishly. "I would really like to sit in the quiet and maybe sleep."

Rebecca frowned. "Again? But you just woke up from a nap. Are you truly that tired?"

"*Jah*, I'm tired. I'm in pain, too." She barely refrained from rolling her eyes. "My leg is broken, sister."

Darla clicked off the remote. "Sorry, dear. Would you like us to leave?"

"I really would." She hated to be so blunt, but anything less wouldn't make them leave.

"Oh." Rebecca frowned. "That's too bad. I thought we could keep you company so you wouldn't be lonely."

"I don't know why you are so concerned about that now. You all practically pushed Simon out of the room."

Her sister raised her eyebrows. "He shouldn't have been here, Amelia."

"Why?"

"You know why."

"Because he's a man? I don't think he was going to try anything untoward. I have a broken leg. Besides, I owe Simon a lot. After all, he was the one who rescued me."

"He shouldn't have been at our farm in the first place," Rebecca retorted. "I told him to stay away from you."

"You shouldn't have told him such things. He wasn't being disrespectful. He wants to court me."

Rebecca bit her lip and looked away.

Frustrated, Amelia turned to her sister-in-law. "What does Lukas think?"

"Oh, well, I probably shouldn't say," Darla said hesitantly.

"This is my life. How would you feel if your siblings were tell-

ing you what to do?" Amelia knew she'd struck a chord. Mere
months ago, Darla's brother Aaron had treated Darla terribly. If
Lukas hadn't stepped in, well, things could have gone very bad.

"Lukas doesn't want Simon courting you," Darla finally said.

"Obviously. But I don't see why Lukas is so against Simon.
Actually, I don't see why my personal relationships are any of
his business."

Darla flushed. "You know how brothers are. They like to interfere."

"I agree, but Lukas is being unreasonable."

"Simon ain't suitable, Amelia," Rebecca said. "I'm sure you've
heard the rumors about him."

"About his *rumspringa*?"

"*Jah,* I'm talking about his *rumspringa*. And everything else,"
Rebecca said. "Simon didn't just go out and watch movies when
he left Charm. He went wild. He drank. He did drugs. Some
people say that he was arrested."

Amelia had actually heard such things, too. She'd done her
best to ignore the rumors. "I'd rather you not gossip about him."

"It's not gossip if I'm voicing my concern. He's too worldly."
After exchanging a glance with Darla, Rebecca said, "The good
news is that he understands now."

"Simon understands what?" she asked slowly. Feeling panicked,
she looked at both women. "What, exactly, did Lukas say?"

Looking increasingly uncomfortable, Darla played with the
folds on her dress. "I'm not sure," she said.

"But whatever he said made an impression," Rebecca said. "I
think Simon understands that he needs to simply be your friend
from now on."

If Amelia could have gotten to her feet and yelled in frustration, she would have. "I really can't believe all of you are focusing on such things today. I'm lying here injured, but all any of you care about is Simon's unsuitable courtship."

Rebecca folded her arms over her chest. "It weren't much of a courtship. He was sneaking around . . . as you know."

"Simon did not sneak."

Darla nodded. "*Jah*. But don't be mad at Lukas, Amelia. He's only doing what is right."

"For who?" Sheer frustration caused her voice to tremble. "Simon took care of me today. He's been nothing but kind to me. And . . . and I think I love him."

"You might think you love him, but you'll meet someone better. Look what happened with me and Jacob."

"Please leave. Both of you."

"Don't be like this."

"Don't be like this? You and Lukas are ruining my life." Picking up the call button, Amelia glared at both of them. "You two need to leave, or I'm going to call the nurse to ask you to leave."

Just as Rebecca looked determined to argue, Darla grabbed her hand. "We'll go now, Amelia, but please try to understand. Lukas loves you so much. And he feels responsible for you since your father is gone."

No, the problem wasn't that she needed to try to understand. What was happening was that she understood too much. For most of their lives, the four of them had been living in each other's pockets. Because of their mother's early death, they'd helped out around the house together. They'd worked at the mill together. Essentially, they'd intertwined their lives around each other so much that it was almost impossible to do anything independently.

But over the last year, Lukas had courted Darla without Levi's blessing. Rebecca had pursued her dream of teaching. And even though that hadn't panned out like she'd hoped, she'd pursued it. Even Levi, their usual carefree brother, had needed a break and gone away.

She, however, had done none of that. Instead of courting or working or, well, complaining, she'd stayed at home and tried to make their lives run as easily as possible. She would have even been relatively content to hold her crush close to her chest. It would have been okay if Simon never realized that he—and only he—made her heart beat a little faster.

But when he'd begun to focus more of his attention on her, she'd known it was time to spread her wings a bit, too. She wanted to follow her dreams as much as her siblings had. The problem was that they weren't used to her ever following her dreams. Certainly not at the expense of their expectations.

Though all of that was running through her head, she was too tired to try and explain herself. She didn't even think they'd listen. Therefore, she simply did whatever she could to get them to leave her alone.

"But Lukas is not my father, and neither of you girls is my mother."

"Amy," Rebecca bit out, "you aren't listening. If you would just see things from—"

"Your point of view?" Amelia finished sarcastically. "I could say the same thing to you. Just know that I'll remember this, Rebecca. I'll remember just how you forced your way into something that wasn't your business." Then she shifted and turned away.

It was childish, she knew, but didn't open her eyes again until she heard the women shuffle out the door.

Then, with a sigh, she adjusted her bed and tried to come up with a plan to get Simon back. He'd promised to return to see her tomorrow. When he came back, she'd thank him for his care, then push a little bit. It was time for the two of them to move forward. To face her family together.

Liking how that sounded, she smiled. She might have been the youngest member of her family, but she was not the weakest.

Lukas and Rebecca were about to discover that.

WHAT DID A person say to a sibling he hadn't seen in years? Simon had no idea. As he sat in the passenger seat of the fancy sports car that Tess was driving, he tried to come to terms with the fact that this Englisher woman was the same girl he'd grown up with.

But so far, the only thing that seemed familiar was the scar on her lip. He didn't dare bring that up, though. He remembered exactly how she'd gotten it.

Instead, he gave her directions to Josephine's Café. It was located in the heart of Charm and was fairly new. With its eclectic décor and bistro-type menu, it was a welcome change from the many home-style restaurants in the area. Most everyone liked it, men and women, Amish and English alike. It seemed the right choice for Tess.

He'd considered letting her choose a place in Millersburg, but then he would have had to depend on her for a ride home. He hadn't wanted to do that.

As they pulled into the parking lot, Tess said, "This place is new, isn't it?"

"Yep. Opened about two years ago."

Still scanning Main Street, Tess frowned. "Wow. A lot has

changed around here. The only place I recognize is Grandma's Homestead Restaurant."

He smiled. "I don't think Grandma's will ever close. You're right, though. Some things around here are fairly different. Others, not so much." Of course, he was talking about more than restaurants.

She nodded. "I guess you are right."

After they got out, she pushed a button on her keys and set the alarm.

"Doubt you have to worry about locking your car here." On either side of her shiny sedan were two late-model farm trucks, one of which had its window partly rolled down. Near the back of the café was a hitching post with a horse and buggy tied up. Her fancy vehicle stood out like a beacon.

"Old habits, I guess." She looked a little chagrined but didn't make a move to unlock her car. Instead, she dropped the keys in the opening of her purse.

"I guess so."

He held the door for her and they walked in. Josephine looked up curiously from some menus she was cleaning. Two tables were filled, one with a pair of Amish women, another with a family of four. Simon gestured to a table near the back wall. "Let's sit over here."

After they sat down, Josephine brought them menus and took their drink orders. Then, as if she sensed that they needed plenty of time alone, she walked away.

"She seems nice," Tess said. "Do you know her?"

"Not so much. It's a *gut* restaurant, but I've never been one to chat with relative strangers."

She smiled softly, fingering the bright purple paint on their table. "I can see that." Raising her chin, she said, "Simon, how do you want to do this? Do you want to know what I've been doing? Do you want to tell me about you?"

"Why don't we order some food first?"

"Oh. Sure." She stared at her menu.

It was strange, but Tess's nervousness made him breathe easier. "I usually get the specials, but people say the soups and salads are good, too."

When Josephine returned with their glasses of water, she said, "I've got chicken parmesan today. It comes with a green salad and garlic bread."

"I'll have that," Simon said.

"Me, too." Tess picked up both of their menus and handed them to Josephine.

"*Danke,*" Jo said, then narrowed her eyes at the two of them. "Hey, you two look almost like brother and sister. You have the same eyes."

Simon grinned. "*Jah,* we do."

When they were alone again, Tess sipped her water. "Tell me about you, Simon. Are you happy?"

"For the most part."

"What do you do?"

"I work at Kinsinger's. I'm a manager there. I bought a little house two years ago. It's not much, but there's only me."

"Do, um, our parents still live in the same place?"

"*Nee.* They moved to a small place over near Berlin."

"Did they not want you to have the farm?"

"There's no way I would have ever gone back there willingly, Tess." Thinking about the cellar and the yelling and the switch their father used to spank him with— Simon chugged back a portion of his drink.

"So, um, nothing changed."

"Did you really think it had?"

She looked down at her lap. "No. But I guess I hoped they would have. And you're still Amish . . ."

"I had nowhere else to go. You and Jeremy said you'd come back for me if you could. You never did." He hated to point that out and didn't wish to make her feel guilty, but he felt like he was barely managing to hold on to himself.

Seeing Tess out of the blue like this was difficult. So many emotions were spinning inside of him. He was happy to see his sister but completely unable let the gaps in their relationship go unnoticed. To make matters worse, he was already feeling stretched to the limit after discovering Amelia in her barn, staying by her side at the hospital, then being told he would never be good enough for her by his best friend in the world.

Why had God decided to heap all of this on him at one time?

"I had every intention of coming to get you, Simon," she said quietly, "but I needed to have a place to take you to, first."

Remembering how scared he'd been on the streets after the initial relief of escaping their house had worn off, he said, "What happened to you?"

"I spent my first three months living on the streets."

He wasn't sure how to accept that statement. "But Jeremy said you were going to be together." That was what Simon had always thought. He'd spent hours imagining the two of them together while he'd been dealing with the consequences of their departure at home.

She shook her head. "We weren't together."

"How come?"

To his amazement, Tess looked apologetic. "Jeremy, well . . . Jeremy hooked up with a bad crowd. They weren't safe."

He almost smiled. "You don't need to shield me, Tess. I have a pretty good feeling what they were like."

"Then you probably will understand what I mean when I tell you that I didn't trust any of them. Actually, I was afraid of most of the guys he hung around. After the first night, I knew I would be safer out on my own."

He stared at her, hard. Even after all this time, her expression was haunted. "So you left?" he asked, his voice softer.

"*Jah.*" She shrugged. "I left the next morning. Jeremy was still asleep." Looking out the window, she said, "At first I thought he might look for me. That he might leave the people he was with . . . but he didn't."

"All this time I thought that the two of you were together."

"That isn't what happened. I only saw him once after I left. It didn't go well. Have you seen him?"

"*Nee.*"

"I'm sorry. I had hoped . . . well, I hoped that Jeremy would have fulfilled his promise better than I did."

She looked sincere. He supposed she was. "It doesn't matter now."

"I think it might," she said softly. "For what it's worth, after things got better, I planned to come find you, but I was too afraid."

"I understand that now." Any reminder of their past was particularly painful.

"Do you? I'm not sure if I do." She stopped and leaned back when Josephine brought their salads. She picked up her fork, then froze when Simon bowed his head.

Then, to his surprise, she bowed her head and joined him in silent prayer.

That action meant the world to him. It helped him realize that they weren't all that different after all. They might have chosen different roads to take with their lives, but they were essentially the same people who had lived across the hall from each other. That realization was all he needed to warm up toward her. "After you left Jeremy what did you do next?"

"I met Jill." Looking happier, she said, "Jill was a police officer when I met her. She brought me turkey subs. Then, one rainy night, she asked me to come home to her house."

"And you did?"

She nodded. "I was afraid, but it was pouring rain. I was sitting in front of a library attempting to stay dry and failing miserably. Jill promised me something better."

"You trusted her?"

"No. But I started thinking that whatever happened with her couldn't be any worse than what already had happened."

Her words hit him in his middle. Amazing how he'd spent the majority of his life never speaking about just how bad things had been at home. Even Lukas knew better than to ever mention his parents. But here, Tess was speaking about the past so plainly. It was difficult to hear. But also strangely freeing. It was as if her willingness to talk lifted some of the burdens he hadn't even realized he was carrying.

Because she was being so brave, he forced himself to ask the question that he wasn't sure he wanted answered. "Was it as bad?"

She set her fork down. "*Nee,* Simon," she said quietly. "She took me into a clean little condominium, gave me an old pair of her sweats, and showed me where my room and bathroom were." Looking as if she still couldn't believe it, she continued. "Then she showed me the lock on the door. She told me to take a hot shower and that when I got out she would have some soup and a grilled cheese sandwich waiting for me."

He swallowed hard. "And did she?"

"*Jah,*" she said, her voice filled with wonder. "I had given up on anyone doing what they said they were going to do. But she did."

When she smiled, Simon did, too. Just in time for their chicken dishes to arrive.

As if she could feel the tension between them, Josephine looked at each of them hesitantly. "I hope you both will like the special."

Picking up her fork again, Tess beamed. "We will. Neither of us . . . well, neither of us ever take meals for granted. Especially not good ones."

After two bites, Simon smiled at Tess. "This is good. I wasn't even sure what chicken parmesan was."

She laughed. "You made a good choice. This is the best I've ever had."

He grinned down at his plate. Because he knew she wasn't talking about the dish, she was talking about the moment.

And she was right. It was one of the best he'd ever had.

But it was too bad that such goodness came on the heels of his necessary breakup with Amelia.

Chapter 6

Walking home just as the sun was setting, Simon stretched his arms out in front of him. This had to have been one of the longest days of his life. First, he'd found Amelia injured on the floor of her barn, then there'd been the ambulance ride and worry over her health. Then, just after he was reeling from his discussion with Lukas, he'd run into Tess.

Now that he was walking back home at last, Simon was feeling more confused about his life than ever.

It had been startling to see how Tess had transformed herself. Instead of the teenager he remembered who'd been both bitter and practically afraid of her own shadow, she'd become strong and compassionate. She seemed successful, too—a woman that she was proud to be.

Had he reached that point yet? Was it even possible?

He had thought so until he'd been completely open with his best friend about his arrest, drug use, and prison sentence. Now Lukas was acting as if he was tainted for life.

Maybe he was.

What would it have been like if someone, anyone, had stepped up for him? It would have been nice to have a Jill in his life.

Then he remembered Mr. Kinsinger. That man had sat across from him in his office and listened to Simon's story without interrupting. Then, before Simon even had to beg, he'd offered him a job and pulled out five one-hundred-dollar bills from a locked drawer in his office.

Mr. Kinsinger had believed in his worth and that had meant more to Simon than even the money he'd needed to find an apartment and get some clothes and food. If Lukas's dad hadn't been there for him? Well, Simon didn't care to guess where he would be now.

Several times, he'd been sure that Tess had wanted to ask him about his current life. She'd been curious about his job and his home.

He wasn't sure why, but he had dodged most of her questions and even refused her offer of a ride home. He needed space; and though he wasn't ashamed of where he lived, he wasn't quite ready to see Tess's expression when she saw just how much work his little farmhouse and adjoining barn needed.

Though Tess had looked disappointed, she hadn't argued. After giving him her cell phone number, she'd reluctantly agreed to split the payment for the meal, gave him a little wave, and asked him to call her sometime soon. He'd promised he would.

Now as he reached the top of one of the rolling hills just to the west of his plot of land, he spied a teenage boy walking on the side of the road. He was kicking at an old soda can that someone had probably tossed out a car window. Simon was about to ignore him and keep walking when he noticed the boy holding his side in a certain, familiar way.

Making a sudden decision, he crossed over to talk to him.

"Hey, you should probably pick up that can and throw it away. You'd get wherever you are going a heap faster."

When the boy lifted his head, Simon nearly gasped. He was wearing a sizable shiner. When he noticed that the boy's knuckles didn't look red or swollen, Simon knew his suspicions had been right. The kid hadn't just gotten out of a fight. He'd been beaten.

To his credit, the boy didn't look away. Instead, he stared at Simon unapologetically. Practically daring him to comment on his appearance.

Simon didn't dare. "We haven't met. My name is Simon Hochstetler."

"I'm not Amish."

No, he wasn't. The boy was wearing faded jeans, tennis shoes, and a white T-shirt. His hair was practically shaved off.

But even if he wasn't Amish, Simon felt like he knew the kid well. "I kinda figured that," he stated, letting his sarcasm shine through in his tone. "So, what's your name?"

Instead of answering, the boy stared at him. Everything in his body language hinted that he was distrustful of Simon. And angry. So angry.

But he didn't run off, either.

Remembering how relieved yet anxious he'd felt whenever he'd escaped his house, Simon said easily, "Even though I'm Amish, I still have ice."

"So?"

"I live right down the street. The old white house with the faded red barn."

For the first time, a spark of interest entered the boy's brown eyes. "You live in the ugly one?"

Simon almost grinned. "*Jah*. It's a real eyesore. Ain't so?"

"How come you haven't fixed it up yet? My parents—I mean, some people say that you should."

"I figure they're right. Want some ice or a compress for your eye?"

He took a step back. "I'm okay."

"Sure? 'Cause I've had my share of black eyes, and I've got to tell you that it's going to feel worse tomorrow if you don't try to get the swelling to go down."

"I'll be fine."

"Have you eaten?" He held up his sack. "I've got half a chicken parmesan dinner in here. You're welcome to it, if you want."

"Why are you being so nice?"

"Because I've been where you are."

The boy looked at him suspiciously. "I don't know what you're talking about."

So tough. So scared to trust. Choosing his words with care, Simon said, "I don't know who got the best of you with his fists. All I know is that my father liked to take his anger out on me. For years. I walked around these streets of Charm any chance I could. Some days I would just be lonely. Some days, I'd be so hungry I could hardly stand it. Other times, I would just be hoping that someone would care enough to notice."

"Did anyone?"

"Nope." Eyeing the teenager carefully, he added, "I guess I just wanted you to know that I noticed."

For a split second, a look of longing so sweet entered the young man's eyes that it practically took Simon's breath away. Then his expression became shuttered again. "I'm not you."

"All right, then." He held out his sack from Josephine's. "Even if you don't want any ice, you're welcome to my leftovers."

"No, thanks. I gotta go."

As Simon watched him turn and walk away, he called out, "Boy, what's your name?"

Though the boy kept walking, he slowed his pace. "Justin."

"Good to meet you, Justin. If you are ever out this way again, stop by and say hello. You can see my place close up."

Justin froze, then started walking again.

Simon smiled. At least he'd been heard. He reckoned that was a start.

Later, when he was walking up his drive, his gaze drifted to the old barn that rested a few hundred yards from his house. It was a large, looming thing. It was a bit lopsided and covered in peeling red paint. Ugly. Since he didn't keep a horse, he'd often thought of tearing it down, but he hadn't had the heart to destroy something that was still useful.

But now, thinking of Justin, he wondered if there was a reason it was on his property. Maybe that barn could be used for something besides housing animals and farm equipment?

"I think I made a really big mistake, Jill," Tess said into her cell phone after filling her in about her surprise meeting with Simon and the meal they shared. "I might have come on too strong."

Jill laughed. "You, Tess?"

Tess flushed. "You know me as a pretty direct girl, but I wasn't always like that. I used to be fairly timid."

"I remember exactly how you used to be," Jill said softly. "You're right. You weren't always so confident."

And just like that, the memories returned. Before she knew it, she was lying on her side on her motel room's queen-sized bed, her legs tucked close . . . just the way she'd gone to sleep in her twin bed in the attic of her childhood home.

Realizing that she was holding one arm protectively around her middle, Tess pushed herself up into a sitting position. Then moved to sit at the desk. Anything to break the memories threatening to overtake her. Feeling a panic attack looming, she closed her eyes and concentrated on breathing in and out.

"Tess? Don't go there," Jill ordered in her ear.

She opened her eyes on an exhale, then realized, to her surprise, that she'd been awkwardly holding the phone to her cheek the whole time. "I'm sorry. Was I panting in your ear?"

"A little bit."

"Sorry. I don't know what happened."

"Don't apologize. I can't imagine how difficult those memories must be."

Rubbing a hand across her forehead, she grimaced. She was sweating like she'd just run a marathon. She pulled up the tail of her shirt and wiped her brow. "I thought I was better."

"You are better. You just haven't forgotten."

"I guess I haven't."

Jill paused, then said in a soft voice, "I remember that little girl who I found in the park real well. That girl was shy and scared and unsure. But there wasn't a thing wrong with her, Tess."

There wasn't a thing wrong with her. How many times had Jill whispered that to her? Likely too many to count. Most of the time she believed it, too. Then, there were moments like today, when she was sure Jill was wrong. When that happened,

Tess would start doubting herself. Worse, she'd remember all the verbal abuse she'd heard at home. All the hateful things her father had told her . . . all the things she'd worried were actually true.

"There still ain't a thing wrong with you. You're a strong and lovely woman. So stop your tears."

Swiping her cheek, Tess laughed. "I don't know how you know what I'm doing and thinking over the phone."

"I was a pretty good cop, girl."

"You were a really good cop." Not only had Jill gone above and beyond the call of duty and rescued her off the streets, she had reached out in countless ways to other members of the community. Over a hundred people had attended her retirement party. "What do you think I should do now?"

"It's not what I think that counts. What do you want to do?"

"I want to see Simon again." Hating how vague that sounded, she said, "No, I want to know Simon again. I want to be a part of his life."

"Then that's what you need to do."

"It's not that easy. What if I see my parents?"

"Just because you see them doesn't mean you have to do a thing," Jill replied, her voice hard. "You owe them nothing."

"What if they want to talk to me?"

"You can either listen to what they have to say or turn and walk away. It's your choice now."

"And Jeremy? What about him? What am I going to do if I see him?"

"Same thing, I reckon."

"You make it sound so easy."

"It's not. But don't forget, he was a victim, too, Tess."

"I know. I'm just not sure if I can handle any more reminders of the past." As soon as she said the words, she swallowed the lump in her throat. She sounded terrible.

"How about you take things one step at a time? Right now, you have something to give thanks for. You got to see your little brother. You even got to share a meal with him."

Leaning back in the chair, Tess smiled. "Oh, Jill, you should have seen him. He's so handsome. And tall! And he's got this air about him, too." She paused, wondering how to describe it. "It's all tough and cool."

"Tough and cool, huh?"

"*Jah*. Like something out of one of those old James Dean movies." Liking the comparison, she said, "Get this. I saw two women on the sidewalk stare at him. I didn't know whether to glare at them for being so brazen or pat him on the back."

Jill chuckled. "You sound like a sister. Like you're proud and appalled, all at the same time."

"I guess I am. I'm still his sister," she said with some surprise. "He's turned out fine, in spite of everything."

"Just like you." There Jill went again. Saying exactly the right thing.

Standing up again, Tess crossed to the window and glanced out. It was dark outside, there was nothing to see, but she wasn't afraid of it anymore. "I had help, though. I had you. I don't know what would have happened to me if you hadn't showed up. Nothing good."

"You helped me, too. Before you came along, all I did was work. You made us a family."

And here came the tears. "I'll never be able to repay you."

"I don't want to be repaid. Love doesn't work that way."

"True, but still . . ."

"When you fall in love . . . if you ever fall in love, you'll understand."

"I'm only thirty-five."

"It's time to let your guard down, girl. Next time some man asks you out to dinner, say yes."

"I'll settle with trying to have supper with Simon again."

Jill chuckled once more. Then, after spending another couple of minutes chatting about Jill's new cat and the yoga class she was taking, they hung up.

Tess wasn't sure what was going to happen next. All she did know was that she had to see Simon again. She needed her brother back in her life. More importantly, she was determined to do whatever she could to keep him there.

That was a vow she was proud of. And a wish she hoped would come true.

Chapter 7

Friday, October 2

The day dawned bright and sunny. As she gazed out the window from her hospital bed, Amelia decided the weather couldn't be more ideal. It suited her mood perfectly. On his morning rounds, the doctor had said that she could go home before noon. Amelia was so happy about that!

She had been worried about being in this large, sterile building. Try as she might, it held nothing but horrible memories for her.

But everyone around her was so kind. They were accommodating and patient. Every time someone walked by, they stopped in and said hello. A few times a day they brought her a cup of cranberry or apple juice. They talked about people they knew or her parents. It seemed most everyone had known either one or both of her parents.

Still, it had been difficult to be polite.

Every time she was alone, her mind would drift back to the

hours she'd spent in the waiting room, hoping and praying that the news about each of her parents would get better instead of progressively worse.

Last night, when the halls had been silent and she could only hear the faint echo of footsteps and voices from the nurses' station, she'd watched the hands on the clock above her bed slowly move around the dial. She didn't sleep a wink.

Now she was watching the door for a whole other reason. Simon had said he'd be back this morning. She couldn't wait to see him. The short time he'd been by her side, she'd been either in pain, afraid, or groggy. Then he'd left suddenly. Now she was anxious to thank him for his quick thinking and care.

She was also looking forward to Lukas and Rebecca apologizing for their efforts to keep Simon away from her. Surely, after witnessing how much she needed him, her siblings would stop all the nonsense about trying to run her life.

But by ten o'clock, she was beginning to lose hope. She knew Simon's schedule as well as her own. He had to be at work by now. Still, she sipped coffee that a volunteer had just brought her and watched the door.

When she heard the steady steps made by men's work boots, she smiled.

Only to see her brother walk through the door.

"Lukas."

At her tone, he stopped and raised his brows. "It's *gut* to see you, too."

"Sorry." She hesitated, then decided to be completely honest. "I've been hoping Simon would stop by. Have you seen him this morning?" she asked hopefully.

"*Nee.*"

"Come on, Lukas. Don't you think it's time we stopped pretending that he and I aren't seeing each other?"

Looking more uncomfortable, he nodded. "*Jah*. I do think we should stop pretending. It's past time."

"If you agree with me, why do you look so put out? You know Simon is a good man."

"Amelia, I'm sorry, but I think it's time you stopped seeing him."

"It's too late for you to decide that. We already are." Completely annoyed, she said, "Lukas, for the record, I think you are being ridiculous. I'm tired of you acting like he is good enough to work at your company but not good enough to court me."

"I'm not *acting* like anything. It's the truth. He ain't good enough for you."

"I think he is." Aware that her hands were trembling with restrained emotion, she added, "Since it's my life that we're discussing and not yours, you need to learn to accept him."

Her handsome older brother looked at the chair beside her, then took a step back and leaned against the wall. "Listen, Amelia," he said slowly, "I know you're upset, but you should trust me on this. Okay?"

"I do trust you. But that doesn't mean you are right. You're wrong about me and Simon."

"You don't know him as well as you think you do."

"I know everything I need to know about Simon."

He pursed his lips, then bit out, "He agrees with me."

She looked away as that statement settled in. Did Simon actually agree with Lukas? Was that why he'd never returned and why he wasn't there now?

But just as quickly, she remembered the tender way he'd held her in the barn. The way she'd catch him gazing at her when no one else was around. He felt something for her. She wouldn't have imagined that. She wouldn't have! Getting angry, she said, "Mamm and Daed taught you better, Lukas. You shouldn't be saying such things to me."

He visibly paled at the mention of their parents. "Mamm and Daed are why I'm trying to do the right thing. Don't you see? They would never want you to be his *frau*." Pushing off from the wall, he continued. "When he and I talked yesterday, I reminded him about his past. He now sees things the way I do."

"What did you do? Threaten his job?"

"Of course not." He sighed. "Simon said he was going to end things today when he comes back to see ya."

Doubt settled in. Her brother was a lot of things, but he wasn't cruel. Had Simon really told him such things? Though each of her brother's words burned, she shook her head. "He wouldn't do that, Lukas."

Looking uncomfortable, he rubbed the back of his neck. "He is, Amy. He should be here soon."

As if Lukas had conjured him up, Simon walked through the doorway just then, looking as handsome as ever. But this time, instead of looking happy to see her, his hazel eyes were filled with worry.

When he saw Lukas standing by her bedside, he stopped. "Hey."

"Simon. We were just talking about you."

"I bet."

"I'm glad you came."

"I told you I would. I keep my promises, Luke."

As Amelia watched their stilted interplay, hurt mixed with

pure irritation. Simon still hadn't looked at her. And here she was, stuck in this bed and forced to watch. "Simon, did you come to see me or my brother?"

Immediately, he turned to her. "You, of course."

She noticed his expression had softened. There, at last, was the warm gaze she loved so much. "Then come closer, wouldja?" When he did just that, she looked over at her brother, who was now leaning against the countertop on the back wall, his arms crossed over his chest. "Lukas, the doctor said I would get discharged around noon. Maybe you could come back then?"

"There's no need. I'll wait."

"I'd rather you didn't."

"Amelia—"

She interrupted. "Simon, maybe you could help me get home?"

He swallowed. "*Nee,* I'm afraid I canna do that."

Perhaps things really were as Lukas said. Simon wasn't asking Lukas to leave them alone. He wasn't reaching out to hold her hand. Actually, though he was standing by her side, he looked rigid. "You can't or you won't?" she asked at last, hating the new thread of doubt in her voice.

"Does it matter?" he asked.

"I think so."

"I'm . . . I'm going to go wait in the lobby, Amelia," Lukas suddenly blurted. "I'll come back in a little while."

When she and Simon were alone, she gestured to the chair by her bed. "Want to sit down next to me?"

"*Jah.* Of course." After taking the chair, he rested his hands on the metal railing. Then, ever so slowly, he scanned the length of her body.

As if he was caressing her, she felt his gaze settle on her leg with its orange cast, then drift to her hands. One was lightly wrapped in gauze because of her snake bite, the other sported a small bandage from her IV. She felt his attention pause on the collar of her blue-and-white-checked hospital gown. Then he let his gaze caress her face, and finally her hair. Of course, she wasn't wearing her *kapp*. Her white-blond hair was neatly pinned, thanks to the volunteer who had come by an hour earlier, but it was likely the first time in years that he'd seen her head uncovered.

She wondered what he thought. All her life, she'd been told she was pretty. Though it was a sin to be prideful, she knew it was true. The Lord had blessed her with pleasing features. But all she'd ever cared about was if Simon thought she was appealing. She so wanted him to want her.

As he stared at her, his own expression softened. She felt him study her so closely, she was sure he was memorizing every one of her features.

She held her breath, unconsciously preparing herself for his praise. Things between them were going to be just fine.

Instead, he exhaled and dropped his hands to his sides. "How was your night?" he asked.

After debating whether to push him to talk about their relationship, she decided to wait. If he wanted to prolong a hard discussion, she could do that, too. "It was long but not terrible. The doctors and nurses here are nice."

"Did you get any sleep?"

She shook her head. "Not much. Like I told you earlier, there are too many memories here."

Slowly, he slipped a hand up and gripped the bar next to her again. "Did you try?"

His voice was so gentle.

"I can sleep today when I get home. I'll sleep better in my own bed, anyway."

"I bet you will." After meeting her gaze again, he straightened and pulled his hand away.

Perhaps it was time, after all, to force their discussion. "Simon, talk to me about your conversation with Lukas."

"He wasna happy that I have been coming over to see you without him being there."

She noticed that he was holding himself still and straight. He wasn't fidgeting, wasn't shifting. "Don't you worry about that," she stated, hoping she sounded more confident than she felt. "I already told him that I was tired of him acting like I was a sullen teenager who doesn't know her own mind. He'll come around."

"It ain't that easy, Amelia."

"It can be if you want it to be." When he still looked doubtful, she added in a rush, "Rebecca will come around, too. Actually, I think she already has."

"Mmm."

He sounded so noncommittal. So confusing. "Simon—"

"Guess what?" he interrupted. "I had supper with my sister yesterday."

"Truly? Well, that's . . . that's wonderful news." She could barely remember his sister. Only that she had dark-brown hair like he did. "I'm sorry, I forgot her name."

"It's Tess. And get this—she's English now and she sells drugs."

"She's a drug dealer?"

"Not bad ones. I'm talking good ones. You know, like the ones doctors prescribe."

She grinned. "I was teasing. I didn't think she was a danger-ous drug dealer, Simon. So, how was your visit?"

His eyes warmed. "Seeing her was good. She gave me her tele-phone number. She wants me to call her soon. I think . . . well, I think we're going to try to see each other now."

"That's great. I hope, when you are ready, you can introduce me to Tess."

But then, just like that, his smile vanished.

"Amelia, I need to tell you something. You see . . . well, talk-ing to Lukas made me realize that my past is always going to be with me. Seeing Tess reminded me that I still have a lot of scars and bad memories about my childhood."

"I'm sorry for that, but I don't understand why you think I would be bothered by your past. I mean, other than being sad that you've had such a difficult time."

He stared at her again. Then, looking pained, he said, "When I was a teenager, I got a couple of tattoos."

Though he'd always kept his sleeves rolled down, she did recall one time seeing some marks on one of his forearms when he was washing his hands. Not wanting to embarrass him, she hadn't asked what they were. Now she supposed they were tat-toos. To her surprise, she realized she wasn't all that shocked. She'd always known that Simon had been a bit rebellious. He'd gotten in trouble more than once at school for talking back to their teacher or not following directions right away. He'd also been the first person in their group to accept dares when it came to doing something outrageous.

Then an image flashed in her mind of him walking slowly through her family's property. He'd looked scared and ashamed, especially when she'd spied his black eye. She would much prefer his skin to be marked with ink of his own choosing than cuts and bruises from another's hand.

But of course she wasn't about to share any of that. "And?"

His eyebrows rose so high, they looked like they were trying to inch off his face. "And? That's all you have to say?"

Of course it wasn't. She wanted to ask about a dozen questions. She wanted to see them, too.

However, if she asked to see them, he would likely refuse. Therefore, she simply shrugged. "I'm not sure what you want me to say, Simon. They're just marks on your skin. That's all."

As she stared at his covered arms, she imagined his tattoos suited him. Simon was such a complex person. So much of his past was carefully hidden or buried deep inside that it seemed rather fitting he would be hiding such marks under his perfectly formfitting shirt.

Furthermore, she felt privileged. He'd just told her something that he hid from the rest of the world. He'd trusted her enough to do that. And because of that, she was remonded again that she didn't have just a simple crush. She loved him.

When he continued to look so ill at ease, she realized that he was waiting for her to speak. "Simon, why did you tell me about your tattoos?"

"I wanted you to know the truth about me. During my *rumspringa,* I . . . well, I didn't stay around here, Amelia."

"I know that. Don't you remember? I saw you the night you ran away."

"You've never mentioned that night. I thought maybe you'd forgotten. You were just a little girl."

"I didn't forget."

After staring at her a moment, he looked away again. "Anyway, after I left, I went down to Columbus and hung out with a lot of guys who did bad things."

"Like what?"

He shrugged. "Sometimes I fought."

"I don't understand."

"I fought in underground clubs, Amelia. I fought for money."

She shook her head. As much as she was hearing him speak, the words he was saying didn't completely register. "Did the people you fought hurt you?"

"Sometimes. But after the second or the third round, I usually won," he said quietly. "I pushed aside everything our church has taught us and embraced violence."

"I see."

He wasn't looking at her now. "I made money and spent it on alcohol and drugs, Amy. And I hung around guys who stole cars. That is why I went to prison."

She was shocked. She'd be lying if she said she hadn't heard one or two girls whisper such stories about him. But she hadn't ever believed it. Now she felt a bit foolish. Had she been falling in love with a man who had embraced everything she'd been taught to scorn? She wondered if Lukas had been right. Maybe she didn't know Simon at all. "Why did you do all that?"

He blinked. "Why?"

"Even though I didn't know about the fights or the drugs or, um, prison, I know you wouldn't have done something like that if you didn't have a reason. Why did you stray so far?"

"At that time in my life, fighting and feeling pain were what I was used to." Sounding as if he was pulling each word out of himself, he said, "First Jeremy left, then Tess a year later. I was left to bear the brunt of my parents' anger."

"Oh, Simon."

Still not meeting her gaze, he continued. "My life at home wasn't a good one. We used to get locked in the cellar when we were bad. And"—he inhaled—"and my father used his fists on me a lot."

It was taking everything she had not to burst into tears for him. For the little boy he'd been. Instead, she forced herself to keep her expression blank and open. She needed to hear what he had to say. But just as importantly, he needed to tell her about his suffering.

"Because of all that," he continued in a strained voice, "I knew how to handle pain. I was angry, too. So angry. God forgive me, but I wanted to hurt someone else." He lifted his chin. "But unlike my father, I wasn't taking out my anger on a child who was weaker than me. I was taking it out on someone who could fight back."

"So that's why you were good at it."

He nodded. "I was good at doing bad things, Amy. But then I got caught and had to pay the price."

She had a lot of questions, but she didn't want to ask them. Not right then. "Why did you come back?"

"Back? I don't understand."

Gently, she said, "Simon, if your brother and sister left our faith, if you made other friends and you were making money fighting, too . . . why did you come back here after you got out of prison? Why did you come back to Charm, start working at the mill, and get baptized in our faith?"

"Because I felt I had to." He swallowed. "I realized that I was only running away, not changing. And, well, one night after a particularly bad fight, I realized that I didn't hurt anymore."

"And then?"

"And then I discovered that I had to stop being so self-destructive. I needed to somehow find some hope in my life." He paused, looking as if he needed a moment to compose himself. "I came to the conclusion that there was only one group of people who could help me be hopeful, and that was the Kinsinger family."

"Because Lukas and Levi were your best friends."

"Because of them, *jah*. And because of you."

She wished she wasn't stuck in this bed. She wished she was brave enough to grab his hands and hold him. To pull him close so she could wrap her arms around his waist and hold him tight. He needed a hug. He needed to remember that he wasn't alone. Not anymore.

"Simon, I am glad you told me about your past. I'm glad you told me about your tattoos. But if you were thinking that I was going to be scared, you are wrong." Feeling that each word might be the most important word she'd ever said in her life, she continued. "I'm not scared of your past. The past is behind ya now. It has nothing to do with us."

"It has everything to do with us. I told you about the things I've done so you would realize that my past will always mark me. I can't remove the scars I've gotten from fights or those tattoos."

She felt like rolling her eyes. Did he really think she was that naïve? "Maybe I don't want you to remove them," she said.

When he blinked in surprise, she almost asked him to roll up his sleeves or even take off his shirt so she could satisfy her curiosity. But of course, that would be terribly shocking.

"Maybe I don't expect you to remove your past. After all, it's already happened. You and me and God know about it. Ain't so?"

"A lot more people know besides the three of us."

"But I don't care what a lot more people say. I only care about you and me and God." Seeking a soothing tone, she said, "Simon, it's obvious that you've already changed your ways. The Lord knows you've repented and feel sorry for any mistakes you've made. That's all He ever asks for. Isn't that enough?"

Looking alarmed, he got to his feet. "You are going to want someone different. One day, you are going to be very glad that we ended things before it was too late."

"You don't know that."

He kept speaking, running over her words. "Because of that, I'm going to end it now."

"But I don't want you to. Don't I get an opinion?"

Looking straight ahead, not meeting her eyes, he added, "I'm sorry, too, for ever going against your family's wishes."

"I am not. I love Lukas and Rebecca, but they don't know what's best for me."

"I'm also sorry that I pursued you and led you to believe that we could have a relationship. I shouldn't have been so forward."

Even though she was lying in bed, she glared at him and attempted to look stern. "I disagree." Trying again, she added, "Simon, don't you see? I get a say, too. I have a mind and an opinion and my own wishes and dreams and regrets. You are not alone in this."

"I understand. However, I feel that your vision of us, well, it's tainted at the moment."

"Tainted?"

"*Jah*. You aren't seeing me for who I am."

"If that is the case, then you aren't seeing the real me, either."

His mouth opened. Shut. He clenched one hand hard. Finally, he sighed. "Look. I need to leave."

He was going to run away. He was going to refuse to listen to her, refuse to change his mind. "I guess you do."

He stepped toward the door. Without looking back at her, he whispered, "Goodbye, Amelia." Pain laced his tone. It was heartbreaking.

It also ignited her temper. "There's no need for goodbyes. I'll see you soon, Simon. I promise you that."

Without saying another word, Simon threw open the door and walked out into the hall.

Amelia watched him leave, realizing that she'd been through a lot of things during her lifetime. She'd lost her mother when she was far too young. Survived her father dying in a terrible way. She'd mourned the deaths of men she'd known and dealt with Levi leaving.

Through it all, she'd done her best to adapt to whatever life had thrown her. She'd made changes. Pushed aside her own wishes and dreams and put her family first.

She'd never regretted those choices. Not until today.

But never had she been so disappointed in her brother and sister. And she'd never been so disappointed in Simon.

He could survive being locked in cellars and street fights and drugs and crime and prison . . . but he couldn't stand by her side and accept her love? She found that hard to come to terms with.

He was obviously right. They did not belong together. It was time she moved on. Even if it hurt to do so, it couldn't hurt worse than she did right at that moment.

Chapter 8

After leaving Amelia's room, though he could care less how Lukas felt, Simon forced himself to go to the visiting area and approach his best friend. Lukas turned the minute he entered the room and watched Simon warily as he approached.

"How did it go?" Lukas asked.

"About how one would expect. Not well. She ain't happy with me. Or with you and her sister."

Lukas nodded. "I figured as much. Thank you for ending things, though. I owe you."

Everything about his words felt wrong. "You don't owe me a thing. And don't ever thank me for doing this. Amelia is upset."

"She'll get over it."

Simon noticed that even as Lukas said the words, he didn't look all that confident. "Maybe." He was just about to walk away when his conscience nagged at him to utter something else. "Just be sure you understand that I did not break up with her for you. I ended things because it's better for her. She deserves someone better than me."

Looking increasingly ill at ease, Lukas said, "I understand."

"Do you?" Suddenly, Simon wasn't sure if he even understood anymore. For the last couple of years, he'd taken to pretending that his past had never happened. Since no one ever asked him about being arrested or living in prison, he'd begun to tell himself that everything he'd done years ago didn't really matter all that much. He'd moved on.

But Tess's reappearance, together with Lukas's unflinching need to protect Amelia, had brought it all back with the force of a runaway freight train. The pain he'd felt at his father's hands felt as fresh as if he'd just received those wounds an hour ago.

It seemed he couldn't run from his past or blot it out. He was going to have to learn to live with the things he'd done. Though he'd intended to simply walk away, Simon knew he couldn't do that anymore.

"My parents used to lock Jeremy, Tess, and myself in the storm cellar when we misbehaved," he blurted. Remembering the damp, musty smell, the spiders and the cold darkness, he added, "There would be shelves of jars of food that we were forbidden to touch. I remember sitting in there, so cold and hungry, and helpless to change my circumstances."

"Did . . . did Jeremy and Tess take care of you then?"

Even after all this time, Simon found he was surprised that Lukas had no idea what his family had been like. Lukas had grown up feeling responsible for his younger siblings. All of them helped each other and always had. With him and Tess and Jeremy? Each of them had learned at an early age to look out only for themselves.

"*Nee*," he answered, hating that his voice sounded so hoarse. "My parents . . . they used to put just one of us in there while the others had to watch."

Lukas winced. "I'm sorry, Simon. I didn't know that."

"You didn't know because I didn't tell anyone. None of us did." He shook his head. "I think I was the only man who didn't have a hard time sleeping in a prison cell. I didn't mind the noise or the light. It's being alone in the dark that gets to me. It still does."

"Your parents were cruel people, Simon. I've never blamed you for leaving them."

For some reason, Simon couldn't stop sharing. "Later, my father used his fists an awful lot. He would stand beside us in church, proclaim his faith, then go home and hit Tess for any made-up reason he could think of." Still remembering how scared he'd been, how despondent his sister had looked, he added, "I grew up angry and ashamed."

Lukas closed his eyes. "My *daed* knew things were bad at your *haus*. I remember he tried to talk to your father once. But shortly after, your *bruder* ran away. He was afraid to get involved after that."

"Jeremy ran because he heard what your father said," Simon admitted. "Your *daed* was the first person to ever refer to Jeremy as a good boy." Before Lukas could apologize for things that were never his doing, Simon added, "As the years went by, my father got angrier and angrier. Not long after Jeremy left, Tess did, too. By the time I left home, I could withstand a lot of pain."

Lukas's hands shook as he pulled off his hat and brushed a chunk of hair from his forehead. "Simon, you don't have to tell me all of this."

Actually, Simon thought he did. He was almost thirty years old and this was the first time he had told anyone just how bad things had been. Even after he was arrested and a social worker had stopped by the jail, looking for reasons to explain why a scrawny Amish boy was so bad and so angry at the world, Simon had never admitted just what things had been like. It had been too hard. Too much. Too real.

Until now, he'd never been strong enough to admit how weak he'd been.

"I survived prison because one day, just a month after I had been incarcerated, a priest came by."

"A priest?"

"He offered to tend to me. I had nothing to lose, so I let him. And you know what?"

"What?" Lukas whispered.

"He helped me see that it was time to forgive myself. He helped me see that God already knew my worst points but loved me, anyway. Over time, he helped me accept that He believed in me, too." Just remembering how awestruck he'd been, Simon felt the muscles in his throat clench. "It was one of the most miraculous moments of my life, and it happened when I thought I had lost everything. Right there inside a prison."

Lukas swallowed. "He sounds like a gift from God."

"He was to me." Forcing himself to continue, Simon said, "Knowing that he and God thought I was worth something helped me survive the rest of my sentence. Their faith helped me come back home. Their belief in me helped me return to our way of life."

"I was glad when you came back."

"And I was glad to be here. To know you. To work at Kinsinger's."

"You know I'm glad you are there, Simon," Lukas said, his light eyes shining with honesty. "You are a good manager. Everyone respects you."

Simon shook his head, because his friend still didn't understand. "Lukas, I know your family has been through an awful lot. Losing both of your parents and the mill accident? Those were terrible things. But they happened to your family. Through it all, you've had each other. You've never been alone. Not really."

"I understand what you're saying. You're right. I have always counted on Levi, Rebecca, and Amelia."

"If you understand, then you might realize what it was like to count you as a friend. To feel like we were almost brothers."

"You are almost a brother to me, Simon. I love you as much as I love Levi."

"*Nee,* Lukas, you don't."

Lukas reached out a hand. "Simon—"

"Yesterday and today? You've reminded me that I'm really no better than my faults. That no matter what I do, I'll never be able to overcome my mistakes. That in your eyes, I'll never be good enough. To you, I'll always be tainted."

His best friend shook his head. "That wasn't my intention. It's just that Amelia—"

"I know." Simon cut him off. "It's just that Amelia will always be better than me. And you're right, I see that now. I would die if she ever looked at me like I was the kid who got locked in a cellar. A girl like her? Well, she deserves a man who is much better than that."

There was nothing left to say. He turned to walk away.

"Wait."

"*Nee.* I think it's time I stopped waiting." He sighed. "I'm going to head back to work now. I'll do the best I can, like I always do. But I need to let you know that I'm going to start looking around for another job."

"You don't have to do that."

"I do. You see, I got to see my sister for the first time in ten years yesterday."

"Tess? How is she?"

"She's beautiful. She's happy. Successful. And she made me realize that anything is possible if I believe it. I wanted to be here in Charm, Lukas. I wanted to work at the mill. I wanted to grow old here, to go fishing with you. To laugh. And, though it pains you to hear it, I wanted more than anything to have Amelia. I've loved her for years."

"You love Amelia." Wonder laced Lukas's voice. "You really do."

Simon couldn't believe that his best friend hadn't believed that until now. Had Lukas really thought so little of him?

"I can't stay and watch some other man take my place," he said. "I can't watch some other man court her and kiss her. I certainly ain't going to watch some other man marry her. I . . . well, I just wanted you to know."

There were tears in Lukas's eyes now. Tears. "Maybe I was too hasty. Maybe I was being stubborn and controlling and stupid." He shook his head. "*Nee,* that ain't right. I know I was," he added, his voice hoarse. "Please, don't leave."

"It is too late. According to you, what's done is done."

"I was wrong."

"Does it really matter? You, Lukas Kinsinger, have single-handedly done what no one has been able to do since I was fifteen years old. You made me feel worthless. And, well, I simply cannot go through that again."

He walked away, wondering if anything he said sank in. Or if it even mattered at all.

LUKAS KNEW HE'D made a great many mistakes in his life. He'd never considered himself perfect or even close to that. But there had been few times in his life when he'd felt like he'd caused another person pain. He felt that way now.

Feeling as if he was walking in a fog, he strode down the hall toward Amelia's hospital room, mentally reviewing every word that Simon had said.

Had he really been that close-minded?

Yes. He had.

Had he truly been that cruel?

Absolutely.

Spying an empty, open room along the way, Lukas darted into it and leaned against the wall.

"Dear *Got*, what do I do now?" he whispered. "I have cast judgment on a good friend when I know that only You and You alone have that right. I have pushed aside a friend's needs because I was only concentrating on myself and my fear. And now I'm going to have to face those consequences with my sister, whom I only sought to protect but still managed to hurt. What do I do?"

Closing his eyes, he swiped the tears that leaked from them, took a ragged breath, and waited, half hoping that he'd hear the Lord's whisper assuring him that things weren't all that bad and that it would be just fine.

But of course he didn't hear that.

He didn't hear any advice, either. He felt nothing. Only the sharp sting of regret.

Turning back to the hall, he walked to Amelia's room with leaden feet.

She was staring blankly into space when he crossed the threshold.

"How are you?" he asked.

"Do you really want to know?" she returned, her voice bitter.

Amelia was wearing an expression he'd never seen before, one he hadn't even known his little sister was capable of wearing. Coming to terms with the fact that he had seriously misjudged his friend, his sister, and his role as her brother, Lukas forced himself to answer her question as he approached. "I do."

"All right, then. I'm upset. And disappointed. And frustrated with myself."

Those were not exactly the responses he'd been expecting. "I thought you were going to be mad at me."

"Why would I be mad at you? Could it be because you interfered in my life and kept it a secret?"

Okay. She was mad. Really mad. Though there wasn't a lot he could say to make amends, he had to try. "Amelia," he began tentatively, "you know—"

"I'm not feeling real eager to hear what you have to say right now, brother."

"You are right," he said quickly. "I shouldn't have interfered. But I only wanted to protect you."

"But you didn't protect me. You did the opposite."

Unable to face the judgment in her eyes, he looked away. He sat quietly, waiting for her anger. It was no less than he deserved, and he was determined to bear it in silence.

But after another minute, all Amelia did was release a ragged breath.

"Lukas, when I get home, I'm not going to be able to help you all that much until I get used to this cast on my leg."

"I don't expect you to do anything but rest and heal. Darla

and Rebecca and I will step in. Everything is going to be fine."

"It won't be fine. Not yet, anyway."

"There's nothing more that we can do," he said soothingly. "Your body needs to heal. And it will. We'll simply take things one step at a time."

"Lukas, I want you to write to Levi and tell him to come home now."

He blinked. "But Levi—"

"And don't you tell me that you have no idea where our brother is. Levi was confused and restless, but he ain't stupid. He would never leave without giving you a note or writing to tell you where he is. He has written, hasn't he?"

He wouldn't have thought it possible, but she was making him feel as guilty as his father used to during a long lecture. "He wrote one letter," he admitted. "I asked him to keep me informed about where he was."

Those blue eyes of hers flashed. At him. "So now the truth comes out yet again. Another bit of information that concerns me that you didn't deem worthy of sharing."

"I wasna trying to keep anything from you. I was honoring a secret. Levi asked me to keep his whereabouts to myself."

Her expression turned flat. "You chose to honor Levi's secret, even though he left all of us. Even though I've been home, working on the farm and house by myself all the time. You were loyal to his wishes. Not mine."

"I didn't think it would help you if you knew."

"You didn't? I see. It seems like you've been making a lot of decisions on my behalf lately, Lukas."

He was starting to panic. "Amelia, years ago, Simon told me some things about his past. I thought it might upset you. However, until today, I didn't know his whole story. Now that I do, I realize that I judged him too harshly."

"That doesn't excuse what you did. Or what Rebecca did."

"It might, if you would let me speak."

"I don't want to talk about him. Not today." Her voice quaked. "Not anytime soon."

"I don't know what you want me to say."

"How about you go tell the hospital staff that I am ready to leave. If you did that, I would be grateful."

"I will. And I'll contact Levi and ask him to come home."

"*Gut,* Lukas." Staring down at her leg, she said, "After he gets settled, I think it's time I did some things on my own."

"Like what?"

"I don't know, which is kind of the problem, ain't it? Here I've been thinking that I was being an important part of our family, taking care of the animals and house. But all it did was separate me from the rest of the world. And make you only see me as a child."

"I never thought of you as a child. What you do is important."

"That's in the past, Lukas," she replied, her voice flat. "I feel like the Lord has been giving me all kinds of signs, but I've chosen to ignore them. I don't want to do that anymore. When my leg is healed, I think I may very well take some time off from my life, too."

"I really hope you don't do that."

"Oh, don't worry," she replied, her voice thick with sarcasm. "I'll be sure to write to someone and tell them where I am . . . as long as they keep it a secret from you."

Her comment stung, but Lukas knew it was no less than he deserved. He'd messed up so much. Betrayed two people who meant the world to him. "I'll go find out how to get you out of here," he mumbled.

Amelia didn't say a word. Only stared at him like she wanted him out of her sight.

As he walked through the door, Lukas wished that his parents were still alive. His mom would have known how to make things right and his father would have made sure he hadn't been such an idiot in the first place.

But now he was going to have to rely on his faith and his wife to get him through and make things better. He hoped that was even possible. Because the pain in his heart showed him that the impossible had just happened.

He actually felt worse than he had the day their father died.

And this time? Well, he had no one to blame but himself.

It was a terrible burden to bear.

Chapter 9

Tuesday, October 6

S orry about Dr. Phillips today, Tess," Gwen, the receptionist at the family practice office said with an apologetic
frown. "He's been short with everyone lately."

Well, that was one way to describe the doctor's behavior.
Others might have said he'd been plain rude.

But she'd learned over the years to not let things like that
bother her too much. Her job was to sell pharmaceuticals, not
make friends. "No reason to apologize," Tess replied. "I'm just
glad he had a few minutes to speak with me."

Gwen looked as if she didn't exactly believe that, but before
she could comment, the phone rang.

Tess waved goodbye and strode out of the office. The moment
she felt the cool fall breeze hit her cheeks, she smiled in relief.

The waiting room had been overheated and filled with coughing, sneezing, sick patients. She'd been asked to wait for over an
hour, and then when she'd finally gone back to visit with the

physician, he'd treated her as if she was wasting his time. She'd barely been able to talk to him about the samples she'd brought before he'd been called away.

Now she was late for her other appointments, and felt like she needed to take a shower in Purell. She smiled tightly at an elderly man walking toward the building as she rushed to her car, which acted as her office. After opening her laptop and recording notes from her unproductive meeting, she checked her phone and winced.

Her manager had both called and texted, wanting to know her latest sales numbers for the week. Unfortunately, she hadn't met any of her goals. Deciding not to delay the inevitable, she picked up her cell phone and dialed. With any luck Jim wouldn't pick up and she could simply leave him a voice mail.

"Tess. It's about time," he said in his usual choppy, rushed way. "I've been waiting to hear from you so I could finish my report. What do you have?"

"Not much, I'm afraid." She stared at the cars surrounding her in the parking lot as she proceeded to tell him all of her bad news.

He interrupted often, making her feel both frustrated and worthless. But that was his management style. Most of the time, she let his comments roll off, remembering that he actually was a decent person. Not the type of person she'd enjoy sharing a meal with, but he was ruthlessly fair.

That said, he didn't pull any punches when he was disappointed.

She listened as long as she could, then did a little interrupting herself. "Sorry, but I've got another meeting, Jim. We'll talk more later." Thirty seconds later, she tossed the phone in the passenger seat and was pulling out of the parking lot.

As she drove down the street and headed toward the highway, Tess wondered why everything that had happened so far that week had felt both frustrating and, well, wrong. Usually rudeness didn't faze her. Most of the time the pressure she felt when trying to make a new sale was exhilarating. It made her work even harder.

Her ability to focus on her goals had been one of the reasons she'd been so successful in her job. Since she still had goals, she intended to continue not letting little things interfere with them. Money wasn't everything, but it bought her a nice place to live and vacations, two things she never took for granted. It also gave her security, which she valued more than just about anything. Experience had proven that no job was always easy. Some days were like this.

So what was wrong?

She knew, of course. It was seeing Simon again. It was driving through Charm and seeing the buggies and the farmhouses and the quiet, slower-paced life.

It was also her honest conversation with Jill. Her foster mother's advice had helped ease her worries. However, it had also made her want to make some changes. She didn't know how or what, exactly. Only that it was time to make them.

Everything she'd taken so much care to keep at bay seemed intent on disrupting her new life. She was starting to feel that she couldn't move forward until she made peace with her past. That meant she needed to stop being so afraid of seeing her parents or running into Jeremy.

It also meant that she needed to now be the best sister she could to Simon. She couldn't change the past, but she could help her future be better. And, with the Lord's help, she could maybe even help Simon with his hopes and dreams. She was simply going to have to keep reaching out to him.

And when she wasn't repairing her past and working on her future?

Why, she had a job to keep.

Thirty minutes later, after she pulled into the next medical park, presented her business card, and asked to speak to the doctor, she almost laughed when the receptionist pointed to the one empty chair in the waiting room. Right between a mother holding a feverish toddler and an older lady who was coughing without covering her mouth.

It was going to be a very long day.

And it was going to be a miracle if she didn't get sick.

To her surprise, she realized that wasn't the worst thing that could happen. Not by a longshot. It was good that she finally remembered that.

THE PROMISE OF snow had sent practically everyone in Charm to the market. As Simon stood in line with his small basket of lunch meat, bread, and canned soup, he wished he would eventually learn to plan his meals ahead of time.

But no matter how hard he tried, he wasn't able to figure out what to buy for the following day's supper. Because of that, he stopped at the market almost every day. Most of the time, he could get in and out in ten or fifteen minutes. Today, with the crowd? He'd be lucky to get home within the hour.

"Guess you couldn't stay away, either," Rebecca Kinsinger said as she joined his line. "The weather reports always make it sound like the sky is about to fall in."

"I'm not here because of that. I am simply a frequent shopper."

Holding up a quart of buttermilk, she smiled tightly. "I promised Lilly I'd make buttermilk cookies tonight with her."

Knowing that Rebecca's adopted daughter had recently lost
both of her parents, Simon was fairly sure that Lilly would love
the chance to make cookies with her. He'd always been jealous
of things like that when he'd been young. "I'm sure she'll be
grateful for your trouble," he said before facing front again.

As the clerk rang the person in line and they all moved up a
few inches, Simon sighed. It was hard enough to converse with
Rebecca at work. Now that he was completely aware of how
much she didn't want him near Amelia, he really didn't have
much to say to her.

"Hey, Simon?"

Reluctantly, he turned around again. *"Jah?"*

"I need to tell you something." Lowering her voice, she said,
"I was wrong."

He tried to think of some shipping problem he would have
talked to her about. "Wrong about what?"

"About you and Amelia. I should have trusted you more."
Stepping closer, she said, "I should have realized how much you
love her . . . and how much she loves you."

Right there in the market, he felt his face turn beet red. Only
Rebecca would speak of his personal business in the middle of
a crowded store. "Any reason you changed your mind, Becky?"

"Jah. Amelia gave me a good talking to. And then . . . well,
I did some thinking. I realized I shouldn't have stuck my nose
where it didn't belong. And I should have trusted you both a
whole lot more."

As the line moved forward, he did, too. Then he realized he
could either hold a grudge or take Rebecca at her word.

"*Danke*," he said. "I appreciate you telling me this."

She sighed in relief then smiled. "*Danke,* Simon."

"You ready, Simon?" the clerk called out.

He almost chuckled as he put his bread and turkey in front of the clerk. "As ready as I'll ever be," he replied.

The clerk looked at him strangely but didn't say a word, only rang in his purchases.

After Simon paid, he nodded to Rebecca. "Be careful going home, Beck. See you tomorrow."

"You, too," she said with a smile.

When he started home, he at last felt lighter of heart. He hadn't needed Rebecca's approval and support. But it sure felt good.

AMELIA HAD NEVER imagined that she'd be entertaining a new suitor so soon after having her heart broken by Simon. But it seemed that God intended for her to be constantly surprised by His will.

Less than an hour ago, and not four full days after Simon had broken up with her, Pierce Brenneman had appeared at their door. After Darla had greeted him warmly, he'd deposited a large wicker basket full of casseroles and baked goods on their kitchen counter. And now? Now he was sauntering— sauntering!—her way.

Darla simply stood and watched, looking amused.

Until that moment, Amelia had never given Pierce much thought. He was quiet and reserved. Polite. He was neither ugly nor especially handsome. He wasn't close to either Levi or Lukas. Not to Simon either, for that matter. Therefore, whenever they crossed paths at church or in town, her eyes skittered over him.

He was kind of the mayonnaise of men: easy to take, but not a person one wanted to be around in large doses.

Actually, if she had thought of him at all, it was only because he had an unusual name. He also had an unusual job. He was a goat farmer. Until she'd acquired Princess, she'd never wondered why a man would choose to spend his days among a herd of wily, inquisitive animals. But now she understood. In fact, Princess might be her favorite member of the family right now.

But as she reclined on the couch and watched Pierce approach, Amelia was starting to wonder if, perhaps, she should have given him a whole lot more thought.

When he stopped directly in front of her, he smiled ever so politely. "Amelia, good afternoon."

She inclined her head. "Good afternoon, Pierce. It's kind of you to stop by."

"My mother made your family several meals, since we figured you wouldn't be able to cook anything."

"That was kind of you, though, as you can see, Darla is doing a fine job." She looked over in Darla's direction and was amused to see that Darla wasn't even attempting to do anything but eavesdrop on her caller.

"I am sure she will do her best. But of course, everyone knows that you are the real cook in your family."

Amelia blinked. She was sure there was a compliment in there somewhere. But as she glanced Darla's way again, it was plain to see that Darla hadn't taken his comment as a compliment.

Waving a hand, she said, "Would you like to sit down for a few minutes?"

He sat. Immediately. Then, leaning forward, he spoke. "Amelia, I have to tell you that I'm always amazed by the Lord's timing."

"Oh?"

"*Jah*. I have been trying to find the best way to approach you. You getting hurt was the perfect way."

Glancing back at Darla, who was now visibly attempting not to snicker, Amelia smiled at Pierce. "*Jah,* our Lord God is a wonder, for sure and for certain."

Staring at her intently, he said, "I'd like to call on you, Amelia. Are you presently entertaining a suitor?"

The question hurt. Her siblings had pushed Simon away. And instead of fighting for her, he'd allowed himself to be pushed. "Not at the moment."

Hope filled his gaze. "Then, may I call on you?"

Oh, but she didn't want to answer him. She had no interest in him but no real reason to discourage his attentions. She didn't dislike him, it was simply that he wasn't the man she wanted. How come he didn't approach Lukas or Rebecca like Simon had? "I suppose so," she said weakly.

"*Danke,* Amelia." Leaning back a bit, he said, "I think we will suit well."

"You do?" Suddenly, she ached for him to give her a reason to want him. What did he see in her that was so desirable? Maybe if she knew, she could start seeing herself by his side.

"But of course. I mean, you are beautiful and sweet." He paused, then added, "Plus you can cook and garden."

"Ah."

"And sew."

"*Jah,* I can sew." It was terrible how he had taken the accomplishments that she'd always been so proud of and transformed them into reasons she was worthy of his attention.

In spite of her determination to push Simon from her mind,

she couldn't help but be reminded of how different Simon's attentions had been. Every time he'd come over, he had encouraged her to stop cooking, gardening, and sewing and simply relax and sit with him. He'd say that all her hard work was already evident. That everything was perfect and she deserved a rest.

And when he'd gazed at her? Though she'd always felt his appreciation, she'd known that he'd seen her as more than just a compilation of pleasing features. She'd been sure that he cared about her. About what made her Amelia.

But Pierce? Well, he seemed fixated on each attribute, almost like he was ticking them off a list.

"And then, there are the goats."

She wasn't following him. "Goats?"

"Well, *jah*. You like yours and I have a whole lot of them." He smiled. "We can care for the herd together one day."

How could she admit that she considered Princess her sweet pet? She loved that goat. She liked petting Princess's soft fur. She thought it was cute how Princess liked to cavort in the fields and play.

She did not, however, intend to spend countless hours herding goats! She also was not pleased that he seemed to take her interest in him for granted.

"I think it's a bit early to discuss herding goats together, don't you?" The moment she heard her question, Amelia felt her cheeks flush. Right after that, she gave thanks that her siblings were not in the room. They'd never let her forget it.

Unfortunately, Pierce simply looked confused. "If you say so, but goats take time."

While Amelia stared at him in wonder, Darla sputtered from

across the room. Obviously, her sister-in-law was finding much humor in this conversation.

It seemed her siblings were going to hear about herding goats after all.

When Amelia turned to glare at her, Darla hastily covered up her chuckle with a tissue. It sounded like a choked cough.

Pierce turned to her. "Are you all right, Darla?"

"I am fine, Pierce. Uh, excuse me, I just choked on something."

Turning back to Amelia, Pierce inhaled. "When I heard you got your goat from Hershberger's, I knew we were meant to be."

Amelia blinked. Tried to think of him in a different way. And, well, thought about Princess. She was a good goat. And if a man could surround himself with lots of goats, that had to say something about him. Didn't it?

"Pierce, let me be blunt. You are rushing things between us."

"Oh. Of course. I suppose we should wait a week or two before informing Lukas of our plans."

She was now speechless.

Turning her head, she sent a beseeching look Darla's way. *Help*, she mouthed.

Immediately, Darla stood up. "Pierce, although all this talk of goats and courting is mighty exciting, we mustn't forget that Amelia needs to rest."

"Oh. *Jah*, of course." After getting to his feet much more slowly, he smiled Amelia's way. "I hope you will be up on your feet soon."

"*Danke*," she replied. She was starting to think he truly had to be one of the strangest conversationalists she'd ever met.

"I'll walk you out," Darla told him.

The moment they disappeared from view, Amelia leaned back on the couch. She didn't like to think negatively, but it sure seemed that everything hopeful in her life had vanished. She'd felt nothing for Pierce. Nothing but mild amusement and a heavy dose of frustration.

When Darla came back, she was grinning broadly. "Well, that was awkward."

"Awkward is putting it mildly."

"I cannot even believe he started talking about herding goats with you." Eyes dancing, she said, "What's worse is I think he was actually surprised you didn't think his words were exciting."

"I suppose it's too much to ask that you keep his comments about goats to yourself?"

"I'm sorry, Amelia. I love you, but I'm not going to be able to keep *that* to myself. It was too funny."

She slumped. "I didn't think so."

Darla giggled again. "Come now. Surely, you can see the humor? I mean, you aren't serious about him, are you?" Before Amelia could answer, she added, "He would drive us all batty in no time. And poor Lukas!"

"Poor Lukas?"

"Well, *jah*. Your brother would lose a tooth from grinding his teeth so much."

Amelia agreed, but she wasn't in any hurry to hear about how Lukas was going to deal—or not deal—with her prospective suitors. All she knew was that more visits like the one she'd just survived were going to be in her immediate future. There were a lot of foolish men in Charm, and not a one of them could hold a candle to Simon.

Feeling dejected, she scooted to the edge of the couch. "Would you please help me get to my room? I think I am ready to lie down."

Darla's amused expression turned to concern. "Of course. Are you not feeling well?"

"Just tired. The pain medicine makes one sleepy."

"Yes, I suppose it does." After helping Amelia get one crutch in place, Darla helped her to her feet, then walked by her side down the hall.

When they got to her temporary bedroom—everyone had decided there was no reason for her to navigate stairs if she didn't have to—Amelia sat down on the bed with a sigh. "*Danke.* Thank you for everything. I hate that you have taken a week's vacation from the post office to nurse me."

"Don't give that a second thought. Things have been slow there, and Amanda is happy for the extra hours."

"But still, you are the best sister-in-law."

"We're family. I'm glad I can help you."

Leaning back, she moved both legs up and yawned. She'd mainly wanted to get some space, but it seemed that she really was tired. "I bet I'll be able to help out more tomorrow or the next day."

Darla paused mid-nod. "There's no hurry. You've been doing so much for the rest of us, we're all happy to help you."

Amelia was sure Darla meant every word, but from her perspective, she felt that her family wasn't actually interested in helping her all that much. Not where it counted. She wanted help fixing her broken heart. But of course, if she mentioned something like that, Darla would attempt to reason with her. And Rebecca and Lukas? They would no doubt accuse her of being melodramatic. "Thanks for your help. I'm sorry, but I don't feel much like talking anymore."

"Oh. Of course." Darla opened her mouth as if to ask a question, but then she shut it quickly. Without another word she left.

As she settled into the quiet, Amelia realized that Simon's absence from her life was going to be even harder to accept than she at first had realized. She'd looked forward to his visits. She'd loved the way he treated her, like she was a grown woman who had opinions he valued . . . but also a woman he was attracted to. She'd liked feeling smart and attractive. She'd enjoyed his attentions tremendously. She'd thought she'd meant something special to him.

It was hard to come to terms with the knowledge that he'd backed off after one conversation with her older brother.

And she was even more upset by the fact that she was stuck at home with not a single thing to do about it.

Chapter 10

Wednesday, October 7

After her last appointment of the day, Tess's cell phone had started ringing. She'd been driving when the first of several important calls came through. Needing to concentrate on everything she was hearing, she'd pulled into a nearby parking lot, opened a few windows, and settled in.

As time passed, she'd unbuckled, propped her laptop on the seat next to her, and started opening documents. After another hour, she'd pulled out a spiral notebook and started taking more notes. By the time she'd finished the last conference call, her hand was developing a cramp.

With a frown, she tossed her pen on the seat and flexed her fingers. She'd already worked almost forty hours this week . . . and it was only Wednesday.

She hated that.

The demands of her job used to excite her. They'd made her feel accomplished, like she was worth something. Like all the evenings of night school and scrimping and saving and struggling had been worth it. But as she'd become more successful, her eagerness to prove herself to everyone around her didn't seem to matter as much. Now it just felt like the only thing she had anymore was work. And just like she'd realized yesterday, the money and work were no longer enough. She needed relationships. Real, meaningful ones that had nothing to do with titles and reputations. She needed her brothers.

Tess carefully saved her files on her hard drive, then shut down her computer. Next, she closed her spiral notebook and calendar and slipped all of it into her rolling briefcase. She blinked and looked around. Tried to get her bearings.

Then she started laughing. To her astonishment, across from the parking lot was a wide, freshly plowed field. In the distant was a large, sprawling white house. Clothes hung on the line next to it. To her right was a sign for Hershberger's market, proclaiming it was the home of the area's best fried pies.

Without meaning to, she'd driven back to Charm.

God truly was all knowing. He'd put her back in the very place she hadn't been able to stop thinking about for two days. It seemed He knew that her business here wasn't done.

The truth was that her visit with Simon had meant something. She'd been so overwhelmed with emotion after their brief meal together, she'd gone back to her hotel room and cried. After she'd dried her tears, she realized that she was not as upset about leaving Charm as she was about making the decision to stay away from Simon.

It was obvious that he resented her for leaving him. It was also plain to see that he didn't expect anything from her. He didn't expect her support or money or even her love.

And that was what was lying so heavy on her heart.

She wanted to love him. She wanted—no, needed—his love, too. And because she was older and because she'd moved away, it was going to be up to her to take the first step.

Which, she was sure, was why the Lord had placed her back in Charm.

Tess had gotten Simon's address. Now, before she changed her mind, she entered it on the GPS icon on her phone and waited for the directions to pop up, telling herself the whole time that if nothing came up that was all right, too.

But in less than a minute, she was informed that she could get to her brother's house in eight minutes.

Her mind spun. What excuse would she have for stopping by unannounced? What if he had a friend over? Should she introduce herself as his sister? What if he didn't want anyone to know who she was? What if he wasn't even home? What would she do then?

Tess, why does any of that matter? a sharp, firm voice whispered inside her head.

That, of course, was the best question of all. Shifting her vehicle into drive, she headed to his house. No matter what happened, she was ready to handle the consequences.

"*Danke, Got,*" she whispered, realizing that the prayer sounded more natural and felt more familiar in Pennsylvania Dutch. Maybe it was because she was back in Amish country. Maybe it was because she'd prayed for guidance and strength nonstop when she was here.

Maybe her faith was simply stronger in her first language.

Whatever the reason, she used those brief eight minutes to pray. God heard her prayers, too. Because by the time she parked outside a small house, she felt at peace.

Whatever happened next was out of her hands. As it had always been, her future was in the Lord's hands all along.

SIMON HAD JUST gotten out everything he needed to make a steak sandwich for supper when he heard the knock at the door. Concerned, he hurried over, already mentally readjusting his night's plans. It had to be someone from the mill.

Though they were closed for the day, things happened. Delivery trucks ran late, people complained. Life happened. Because he was within easy walking distance to the mill—and because he had no other obligations—he'd become the first manager to contact if one was needed.

Walking to the door, he wondered who had gotten sent over. He half hoped it was Peter Beachy. He liked that kid.

But when he threw the door open, his mind went blank.

"Tess?"

"Yes. Um, hi, Simon." She looked at him before averting her eyes and quickly scanning the area behind him. Then she met his gaze again.

It was obvious that she was finding it hard to look at him. If that was the case, why had she even come? "What are you doing here?"

The last traces of her smile disappeared. "You know what? I'm not really sure. But I knew I wanted to see you. Do ya mind?"

Her voice wasn't near as sharp as it had been when they'd talked at Josephine's Café. Now she sounded a whole lot more like the girl he remembered.

"I don't mind."

"Ah. *Gut*. I'm . . . well, I'm glad."

Her uncertainty eased the tension that had formed in his

shoulders more than anything else ever could. Stepping backward, he gestured for her to come inside. "In that case, you might as well join me, *jah*?"

"Join you doing what?" she asked as she crossed the threshold and placed her purse on the floor.

He picked it up easily and plopped it on a chair, then led the way to his small kitchen. "I'm making steak sandwiches. Want one?"

"Do you have enough for two?"

He thought that question, along with her tentativeness, was strange. However, it almost made him feel better about himself. He didn't want her to be nervous around him, but he didn't want to be on uneven ground with her, either. She was educated and put-together and smart.

He was none of those things.

"Even if I didn't have enough, I would still share with you. You're my sister."

She inhaled. "You still think of me that way?"

There was a hesitancy in her voice that brought him up short. "Of course I do," he said. "It's what you are."

"You really believe that, don't you?"

"I do." He wasn't sure what else to say about that. Maybe it was because he'd witnessed how close the Kinsinger siblings were . . . or maybe it was because his time in prison had made him learn to never take any relationship for granted. Whatever the reason, he'd learned to simply accept what couldn't be changed—especially if it wasn't something he wanted to change.

She stepped closer. "Hey, Simon. Do ya think one day that we will be able to go back to how we once were?"

"Nee." When he heard her breath hitch, he added quickly,

"But I'd like to think that we could maybe become something new."

"I'd like that." When they got to his little kitchen, she pulled off her jacket, walked to the sink, and washed her hands. "I like your place."

"*Danke.*"

About five years ago, Simon had made an agreement with one of the workers at the mill. In exchange for Simon's upkeep, he paid only half rent for the house. The other half went into a savings account at the bank. Two years later, that money, together with as much overtime pay as he could get, was enough for a down payment.

Now he was actually proud of his house and small farm, though he only had four acres. The house was rather small by Amish farmhouse standards, but it was perfect. The house was well built and had two fireplaces. It also had three bedrooms, one living area, one bathroom, and a large kitchen that ran the length of the house. Since buying the house, he'd replaced the old, peeling linoleum floor with thick oak planks.

Though he'd doubted he'd ever marry, he always liked the idea of giving his wife a lovely, expansive kitchen like this. Any woman would enjoy the counter space and many cabinets. On one side of the kitchen, there was a stone fireplace and a cozy table. If he ever had a family, there would be enough space for two or three *kinner*. The children could sit in warmth while watching their mother prepare them something tasty on Sunday mornings.

But seeing it all through Tess's wide eyes, he felt a little embarrassed. No doubt it was all too obvious that he'd been attempting to reproduce a childish fantasy with such a kitchen.

Not that the rest of the house was much better. The whole thing was only about a thousand square feet.

"It's not real big, but there's only me. You know how that goes. You can only be in one room at a time."

"This is true. But it seems plenty big for you. At least for now, *jah*? I bet one day soon you'll be wanting to get married and have a house full of *kinner*."

He looked at her sharply, unsure if she was being sarcastic. When he saw that she was simply stating things the way she saw them, he relaxed. But that didn't mean he was in any hurry to take up that conversational strand. All thoughts of marriage led him to Amelia, and he definitely did not want to go down that path.

"Do you have a *haus,* too?"

"A condo north of Columbus. It's about the same size as this place." Running a hand along one of the laminate countertops, she said, "It's just newer."

"Kinsinger installs a lot of cabinets and custom flooring in both Columbus and Cleveland, Tess. I'm guessing it's a lot fancier, too."

"Maybe it is," she mused. Running her hand the length of a granite countertop—his latest splurge—she smiled at him. "This kitchen is what dreams are made of."

He shrugged, both hating and feeling relieved that she understood. "I like it here."

"You should. You have everything you need, though."

At one time, he'd thought so. But now, of course, he was thinking that he needed something more.

Pulling open a drawer, he got out his best knife. "I'll slice the steak if you want to toast bread."

"I can do that."

"The cutting board and bread is over there."

She hesitated a moment, then pulled out the fresh loaf he'd bought at the market, located his serrated knife, and began carving thick slices. After pausing, she walked to the oven and turned on the broiler. "I can't believe I just looked for the toaster," she said sheepishly.

"You still remember how to light the stove, though." He pointed to a thin drawer under the oven. "Pans are there."

As she worked on toasting the bread, he pulled out lettuce, tomatoes, and onions and a container of potato salad that he'd picked up at the store, too. It wasn't as good as the potato salad at the Der Dutchman, but it was good.

Ten minutes later they were seated side by side at his small wooden table in the corner. Thick sandwiches and potato salad were on their plates. Glasses of cold milk sat next to each one.

"This looks like a feast," she said with a smile.

"It looks *gut* enough, I think," he said easily. "*Gut* enough for a Wednesday supper."

She smiled at him before bowing her head. When he prayed, he gave thanks for the food and for his day. And for this chance to reconnect with his sister.

She took the first bite. "This is good. Thanks, Simon."

He waved off her thanks. "Tess, are you going to stay in the area tonight?"

"I hadn't planned on it, but I think so. After we visit, I'll go find a hotel. I heard there's a couple of new fancy ones around. Or the B&B here might have room."

"I have room," he blurted before he overthought things and stopped himself.

Eyes wide, she said, "You mean that?"

He nodded. "I think, well, I think it might be a good thing for us to sleep under the same roof again."

"Then I'll stay."

Simon wondered if the tone he heard was relief or merely acceptance. Then he decided it didn't really matter. There had been times in his life when relief came well before acceptance and long before true happiness formed. He didn't know if that was the way of the world or if it was simply how things happened.

He took another bite of his sandwich and forced himself to relax and enjoy the moment. It was nice not to have to eat alone. And now that everything with Amelia had fallen apart, it looked like Tess's company was going to be the only female company he was going to have for quite a while.

"Tell me about your job, Simon."

"Well, you know I work at Kinsinger's." When she nodded, he said, "I'm a manager of one of the warehouses." He was actually more than that. He was essentially the assistant manager, second only to Lukas now that Levi was gone.

"A manager. That's great. Do you like it?"

"*Jah.* For the most part I do, anyway. Of course, I've worked there so long, I think I would have a difficult time doing anything else."

After she polished off the last of the sandwich, she pushed the plate away and crossed her legs. "Are you still good friends with Lukas and Levi?"

"*Jah,* though more with Lukas these days, I guess. Levi took off a few months ago."

"Why?"

He shrugged. "I don't know, not really. Lukas and Amelia

told me that Levi felt he needed a few months' break. After the fire and their father's death, he was feeling like everything was too much."

"Wait a minute. Fire? And Mr. Kinsinger died? What about you?" she asked in a rush. "Were you hurt, too?"

Seeing how alarmed she was, he cursed his tongue. "Sorry. I forgot that you wouldn't have known about all this. Last December, a fire broke out at the mill in one of the warehouses. Five men died, Mr. Kinsinger being one of them. I wasn't hurt, though."

"I'm thankful for that."

Everything in her voice and expression showed that she meant it. There was that lump in his throat again. He cleared it, hoping to control the emotions he couldn't seem to keep at bay whenever he was with her. "I'm, ah, thankful, too. But even though I wasn't hurt, a lot of us have been having a difficult time dealing with it all. It's been a hard time . . . for the Kinsingers most of all. Lukas jumped right into his *daed*'s role while Levi decided to take a leave of absence."

"I can understand him doing that, but I bet Lukas didn't care for his brother's decision."

"I wouldn't have thought so, but he's never really complained too much about it." Leaning back in his chair, he said, "I have a feeling Lukas might understand Levi's need to take a break from his life more than anyone. They have a lot of employees and are under a lot of pressure."

"Are any of the Kinsingers married?"

"*Jah*. Lukas married Darla Kurtz a couple of months ago. Do you remember the Kurtz family?"

She smiled sheepishly. "Kind of. It's all kind of a blur."

"I'm not surprised. Well, Darla was the oldest of seven. She and Lukas have been friends forever. Rebecca was recently married to a man who moved up here from Pinecraft."

"Then, Levi is on his walkabout. And Amelia?"

He swallowed. "She's not married."

"Are you two close?" She suddenly smiled. "She used to have such a crush on you. Do you remember?"

"I remember." He seemed to remember everything where Amelia was concerned. "We are close now. Well, kind of."

"You like her, don't you?"

He should lie, but he was tired of pretending he didn't have a heart like everyone else. "*Jah*. I do." Uncomfortable with both the conversation and the feeling that he was suddenly back in grade school, he pushed away from the table and stood up. Picking up both of their plates, he said, "We should clean up and get you settled."

Tess easily cleared their glasses and then grabbed a dishtowel. "You wash. I'll dry."

"Deal." Starting the faucet, he squirted dish soap and ran the hot water over the plates, wiping them with a soapy sponge.

"Does Amelia not like you?"

"I think she does." He hesitated again, then decided to be completely honest. After all, if anyone would understand, it would be her. "*Nee*. That ain't right. I know she does."

"Then why aren't you all smiles? I don't remember a lot about Amelia, but I do remember that even when she was a little girl, she was beautiful."

"She's still that way."

Tess tilted her head to one side, studying him. "You're handsome, too. What's the problem?"

"Lukas and Rebecca ain't real happy with my past."

"What past?"

"You and I both know I wasn't an angel during my *rum-springa*."

"I doubt your friends were, either."

"You know what they are referring to. About me being arrested and spending almost a year in prison."

"But you were baptized. Your sins were forgiven."

"The Lord has forgiven me, but that doesn't mean Amelia's family wants someone like me tainting a sweet girl like her."

"That's ridiculous!"

"They have a point. I've got a past and even have the ink in my skin to remind me of it the rest of my days."

"Oh, who cares about that?"

He didn't think it was possible, but he felt like chuckling. "They do."

"They are lucky you are alive, Simon," she said, her voice full of an emotion she didn't even seem to be attempting to suppress. "The things you had to endure? Well, a weaker person wouldn't have survived."

Against his will, Simon realized that she was giving him the words he'd been craving. "I thought so, too. But I guess my tattoos aren't the only things that aren't going to fade. No matter what I do, my past isn't going to go away."

"There are other girls."

"This is true." But there was only one woman who had claimed his heart.

He turned off the water and faced Tess. "The other day when I came home, I came across a kid. An English kid. He had a black eye and was holding his side like someone had kicked him."

Her gaze was wary again. "What happened to him?"

"You know what was wrong."

"What did you do?"

"I went over to talk to him. At first, he tried to ignore me, but I didn't give up. I offered to give him some ice for his face."

She sat up straight. "Did he take you up on it?" Her tone was now full of hope.

"*Nee*. He looked like he was thinking about it, though." Grabbing a plate, he started drying it. "I told him he could stop by anytime he needed someone to talk to."

"That's nice of you."

"Maybe." He shrugged. "You know how it is."

She looked down at her feet. "I wouldn't have told anyone anything."

"Me, neither. Well, not the first time. But later, I might have," he added. When his sister raised her chin again and looked at him with wide eyes, he smiled slightly. "Guess what? When he was running off, I asked him for his name."

"Did he give it to you?"

"*Jah*. It's Justin."

"That means he's starting to trust you."

"I hope so. I'd like to be someone a kid like him could trust."

"I think you already are."

Turning to the small kitchen window, he pointed at the rundown barn. "Tess, I've been thinking about the barn on the back of my property."

She walked to his side. "I noticed it when I drove up here. It looks like it's in pretty bad shape."

"It looks worse than it is. Inside, it's sound."

Watching him intently, she said, "What about it?"

"I was thinking maybe I could make it into something for teenagers."

"Like what?"

"I don't know. Like a safe place or something." His words felt stilted because he was still formulating his plan. "I can't help but wonder what things would have been like for us if there had been a place for us to go."

"Jill found me."

"And I eventually went to prison." Remembering too much, he shook his head. "I don't know what would have happened to me if I hadn't gotten arrested."

"Are you saying that prison helped you?"

He grinned. "I wouldn't go that far. But it wasn't all bad, you know? For the first time in over a year, I knew I was going to have something to eat and someplace to sleep." He hated how pathetic that made him sound. However, he was determined to be honest with her. No, honest with himself.

"That counts for a lot."

He was glad she understood. "I keep thinking about Jeremy."

"Me, too." A vacant, lost look appeared in her eyes before she blinked. "Simon, would you have gone to some man's barn here in Charm?"

"I would if I knew the man wasn't going to yell or hit me. I would if I knew he wasn't going to lock me in a dark cellar. What about you?"

The dark shadows that filled his memories flickered in her eyes. A muscle in her jaw twitched before she visibly regained her composure. "I don't know if I would have gone to a stranger's barn or not. Maybe I would have."

"Even if I never went, I would have liked knowing that someone cared."

"*Jah.* That would have been nice." After staring at him hard, she slowly nodded. "Are you going to do something with the barn, then?"

He shrugged. "Like I said, I'm thinking about it. I don't want to make a place to encourage kids to disrespect their parents. But maybe they need someplace to go sometimes . . . just in case. Don't you think?"

"*Jah.*" She turned to stare at the barn again. "Can I help you?"

"Does . . . does that mean you ain't going to disappear on me again?" he asked.

"It does, if you want to know me."

"I want to know you."

As if he'd just given her the best gift in the world, she smiled. It lit up her whole face and warmed his heart. "From now on, I want us to be there for each other, Simon. From now on, all you have to do is let me know you need me and I'll be there. But, hey, Simon? Do me a favor, would you?"

"Anything."

"Don't give up on Amelia Kinsinger."

"I'm not giving up. She doesn't want me."

"I think she does. She is working through it." Tentatively, she wrapped a hand around his bicep. "She's young and she's sheltered. And maybe, in her own way, just as scarred by her past as we are." Lowering her voice to almost a whisper, she added, "Everyone needs a second chance, you know."

"Maybe they do."

"Go call on her. It can't hurt, right?"

It probably would hurt his heart, but Tess did have a point. Amelia meant more to him than just about anything. And that meant that he couldn't give up on her. "I'll call on her again soon."

"Not soon. Tomorrow."

He sighed. "Fine. Tomorrow."

Looking pleased, Tess said, "Now you can show me my room for the night and then take me out to that barn."

"I can do that. I'll do whatever you want."

Chapter 11

Thursday, October 8

Lukas stared at the neatly folded letter that had been nestled in the bottom drawer of his desk since the day it had arrived. After telling himself that he needed to be bigger than his weaknesses, he opened it up and read Levi's short letter again.

Hi Lukas,

As promised, I am checking in. I'm in Florida and am working construction. I didn't want to chance seeing anyone I know in Pinecraft, so I got hired on with a crew that mainly does work in commercial buildings on some of the outlying islands and keys.

The work is hard. Half the time, I'm working outside and it's as hot as you might expect. After the first week, I got the hang of it, though. I drink gallons of water, slather on sunscreen, and keep my head down.

You'd be impressed with my new ability to take directions, too. I'm so glad not to have the responsibility of a whole company on my shoulders that I have dived into crew work. I don't ask a bunch of questions. Simply listen and do what I'm told. My crew leader seems to be impressed with my work ethic!

If only Daed could witness that.

Lukas read that again and found himself smiling. Yes, their father would have been quite entertained to see his bullheaded youngest son transformed into an obedient, quiet worker who asked no questions.

Smoothing out the letter, he read some more.

Lukas, I know I left you in a bind at the mill. I know there's more work than ever to do and you need every hand available. I feel bad about that. We both know that you need me to manage shipping and receiving.

However, after witnessing how Darla's brother Aaron took out his frustrations and anger on his siblings, I decided that gaining some distance wouldn't be a bad thing. Of course, I would never harm our sisters, but I don't trust myself at the moment. I've become a bit short tempered and hard. I need to get back to myself. Until that happens, I know I'm gonna feel as if an integral part of me has gone missing. I dream about the fire but have nightmares about causing an accident that harms men who report to me.

I couldn't survive if a nightmare like that came true.

That has been hard to come to grips with. You are the strongest man I know, Lukas. It's hard for me to realize that I'll never be the man you are.

I don't know if I'll find the missing parts of me here in

Pinecraft, but I do know that I'm so tired and sore at the
end of each day that I don't care. All I yearn to do is sleep.

In closing, be assured that I will come back. I am
planning to return in six months. That said, if you need me,
all you have to do is let me know. I'll drop everything and be
there right away. I might be trying to find myself, but I don't
need to be reminded that you, Rebecca, and Amelia are the
most important people in my life.

I don't know if any of this makes sense. Maybe it does.
Maybe it doesn't. All I can say is that I hope one day you will
forgive me.

Below is my contact info.

Levi.

Just like the first time he'd read the note, Lukas felt a knot in
his throat. His brother's words were open and honest. Levi had
also admitted some of Lukas's darkest fears. What was different,
however, was that his brother was strong enough to admit them
while Lukas was too afraid to be considered weak.

Lukas wasn't sure why he'd never told Rebecca or Amelia that
he'd sent Levi a couple of letters, just to keep him informed of
things. He should have.

He should have also shared Levi's note with them. He had his
reasons, though.

Mainly, it was because Levi's words had resonated with him.
After the fire, he, too, had felt as if he was missing a part of himself. Luckily, he had found enough of that missing part in Darla.

But what if he'd never had Darla? What if she hadn't been by
his side, easing his worries and allowing him to just be "Lukas"?
He was pretty sure he would have buckled under the pressure.

Rebecca, on the other hand, had thought she needed to get away from the mill and do something else. It was only when she'd been allowed to spread her wings and volunteer at Charm School that she'd realized she was happiest doing exactly what she'd been doing.

Lukas had worried that Amelia was struggling just as much as the rest of them. And now that he realized Simon had been the only one she'd trusted enough to lean on, Lukas knew he'd made a bad mistake. He should have thought more about the ramifications of his actions.

He should have discussed his concerns about Amelia and Simon with Levi. He and Levi had always bounced ideas off each other. Their give and take had helped each of them in countless ways. When Levi had left, he'd lost that.

Maybe he needed Levi to come home as much as Amelia did.

He'd pulled out the letter, intending to reread it, then write a letter of his own and mail it off, but suddenly he felt a new urgency. Picking up his office phone, he punched in Levi's construction company's phone number.

A receptionist picked up the phone. "May I help you?"

"Yes. I need to leave a message for Levi Kinsinger, if he is still working there?"

"Levi? Yes, he is. He has a voice mail. Shall I connect?"

"Yes. Thank you." Seconds later, he heard Levi's voice mail recording.

The moment he heard a beep, he said, "Levi, it's me. Listen, Amelia had an accident. It's nothing serious, but she was in the hospital overnight. And, well, she asked for you. She wants you to come home." He paused, then forced himself to say the rest. "I'd like you to come back, too. I've understood why you needed to get away. So I hope you'll understand why I need you back. Thanks."

When he hung up, Lukas returned the letter to the drawer and forced himself to leave his office. If he stayed in there much longer, he was going to dwell on all the other ways he might have messed things up, and that wasn't good.

Seeing Rebecca busily working at the reception desk, he wandered her way.

She looked up in surprise. "Hiya."

"Hi." Resting his elbows on the countertop, he took in the stack of papers, folders, and calendars in front of her. He had yet to figure out how his sister could continually make so much happen out of so much clutter. "How's it going?"

"Busy." She pointed to the visitor log, where vendors signed in. "Lots of meetings are going on today. Every time I look up, someone else with an appointment is walking through the door."

Feeling instantly more at ease, Lukas nodded. Work issues were far easier to understand than personal ones. "Everyone needs to get their inventories set before Christmas."

"They're doing that, for sure. I think we might have a record year, Lukas."

She didn't look all that excited about it, though. Actually, she looked more jumpy than usual, which was saying a lot. His sister Rebecca rarely sat still. Her fingers were absently playing with the pencils on her desk, stacking and unstacking them. She looked agitated, too, and he was fairly sure it had nothing to do with work.

"Anything else going on?" he asked tentatively. "Have you talked to Darla or Amelia today?"

"Darla stopped by on her way to the store."

"Really?" Unable to help himself, he glanced out the front office window. "Is she nearby? She didn't stop by to see me. Is something wrong?"

"Not at all. She wanted to get some egg noodles to make Amelia some fresh soup. She also wanted to share that Pierce came by again."

"He visited for the second time in two days? That's kind of pushy."

Rebecca grinned. "I thought so. According to your wife, he's stopping by early so he doesn't upset our evening routines."

"What evening routines?" Lukas worked at the mill and then he worked at home.

She chuckled. "I said the same thing. He's persistent, I'll give him that."

"I think he's taking advantage of the fact that she doesn't have her parents or brothers there to make sure he stays in line." He normally would never use his position at the mill for personal reasons, but he was starting to think there was a time for everything.

It irked him to no end that Pierce wasn't an employee at the mill. If he had been, Lukas would already be walking his way to give him a piece of his mind. As it was, he had no way to monitor or even attempt to control the man's behavior with his sister.

Not that he'd ever again tell Amelia that he thought she needed monitoring.

"He's a wily one, for sure and for certain. Eager for Amelia's attentions, too."

"Too eager."

With a little sigh, she looked him in the eye. "Lukas, I'm just going to say it. I don't like Pierce courting Amelia. They ain't a good match."

"You're right about that." Though there were a couple of reasons he'd never been a big fan of Pierce Brenneman, he only shared the most obvious. "He's kind of weak."

"He's weak and sneaky. And he talks too much, too."

Lukas grinned. "Huh."

"Oh, stop. I know I talk a lot, but that man is going to drive me crazy if we have to share meals with him on a regular basis. And what if he joins our family?" Before he could comment, she waved a hand. "We have nothing in common."

"He's courting Amelia, not us," he said mildly. "Ain't so?"

"That's the problem. I don't think he's actually interested in Amelia."

"Of course he is."

"*Jah,* but I get the sense that he is also courting us. He takes time to chat with me. He's talked about you like you are something mighty special."

"I'm not?" he teased.

"Not that special," she retorted. "I think Pierce likes Amelia but really likes the idea of being a part of the Kinsinger family." She wrinkled her nose. "I hate that. Our sister deserves more than that."

"I completely agree. I, also, ain't a real fan of his, but we don't want to jump to conclusions."

"But what if I'm right, Lukas? We need to protect her."

"Last time we tried to protect her, it didn't end well. We should stay out of her love life."

"Because of Simon?"

"Of course because of Simon. We pushed him away. We can't push Pierce away, too. Amelia will get mad."

Rebecca frowned. "I kind of think she has reason to be mad at us already."

"I know."

"And, since we're confessing our transgressions . . . well, I should tell you that I think we made a mistake with Simon," she added in a rush.

"I've been thinking that, too."

"Simon loves Amelia. Her—not her beauty or her family's name. I think he would love her even if her last name was Miller and she was homely."

"He's loved her for years." Unable to stop himself, Lukas remembered how devastated Simon had looked when Lukas had told him that he'd never be good enough.

How could he have been so cruel?

How could he have interfered like he had? If his siblings had stepped in between him and Darla, he would have been irate.

Furthermore, Simon was his best friend.

Rebecca was still fussing with pencils and chastising them both. "I know we were worried about his past, but that was unfair."

"I feel the same way."

"Since we're in agreement, what do you think we should do?"

"Nothing. I know Simon. He'll come around. He's tough and determined. He might have backed off, but he's not going to let our interference ruin his future. He ain't that kind of man."

"I'm not so sure about that. Amelia got mad at him. I don't think he's going to risk her being upset with him again." After moving some of the piles of paper on her desk into even more piles, she said, "She loves him and I treated her like a teenager who doesn't know her own heart."

"Did she tell you that she's in love?"

A line formed between her brows. "Not directly, but she alluded to it. She's got a broken leg and a broken heart, too."

"That's a little dramatic."

"Doesn't mean it isn't true."

"What do we do?"

"You need to go take a walk down to the warehouse, locate Simon, and ask to talk to him."

"I don't want to have this discussion on company time."

"Stop being such a worrywart. You run the company, Lukas. You should be able to talk to one of the two hundred employees about whatever you want."

"Your name is Kinsinger, too. Want to come along? Mercy could take over here for a while . . ." Simon might be a little kinder if Rebecca was standing by Lukas's side.

Just then the phone rang. She snatched up the receiver with a relieved grin. "Sorry, I'm simply far too busy," she whispered before clicking onto the line. "You have reached Kinsinger Lumber. How may I help you?"

He turned, went out the door, and started walking toward the back warehouses. Rebecca was right. Even if this wasn't the best time, it was time. And that was going to have to be good enough.

Uh-oh. The boss is coming," Trent, the youngest member on Simon's team, said under his breath.

Simon glanced up from his clipboard and looked down the crowded, narrow aisle in the back of Warehouse Four. Sure enough, there was Lukas walking toward them. He barely glanced at anything around him. Instead, Lukas looked completely focused on one thing: him.

"Did you know he was stopping by today?" Trent asked anxiously. "Is he doing evaluations or something?"

The boy couldn't get it through his head that Kinsinger's didn't work that way. Lukas didn't have time to trot around the facility doing inspections.

"*Nee,* I didn't know he was coming. It's a surprise." And not a welcome one.

Trent brushed back a chunk of the bangs that always seemed to settle over his eyes. "He don't look real happy, Simon. Did we do something wrong?"

"Not that I'm aware of." Knowing that Trent was moments from imagining every worst-case scenario, Simon set down his clipboard. "It's probably nothing," he stated, doing his best to look completely calm. "Go on and take your break."

Trent removed his safety goggles. "You sure?"

"Positive. Actually, tell everyone to take a break now. A semi from Michigan is scheduled to arrive in an hour. We're going to need all hands on deck when it gets here."

"Will do. And hang in there."

"*Danke,*" Simon said wryly. That kid really did crack him up. He was a thirty-year-old in an eighteen-year-old's body.

The moment he was standing alone, Simon let his guard down. He was done with trying to be something he wasn't and had given up trying to impress Lukas. He now knew that there was nothing he could do to improve Lukas's opinion of him. It was a bitter pill to swallow but, like most bitter pills, he felt better now that he'd put it behind him.

Lukas stood awkwardly in front of him. It was obvious that his friend was attempting to find the right words; it was so out of character. Simon would have once tried to help him along.

But not any longer.

"Are you free to talk right now?" Lukas at last blurted.

Instead of pointing out that he'd just cleared the warehouse of workers so they could talk, Simon nodded.

"I need to tell you something."

"Okay."

Lukas's jaw worked. "Problem is, I don't know the right way to say it."

Surprised, Simon tilted his head to one side. "If you don't know, you should probably just go ahead and tell me."

Lukas exhaled, glanced around to make sure they were alone, then said, "I was wrong about you and Amelia. I shouldn't have interfered."

As far as apologies went, Simon figured it had left a lot to be desired. However, as far as surprises went, it was a good one. "What led you to that conclusion?"

Looking even more uncomfortable, Lukas grunted. "Could be that Amelia has been mighty unhappy with me. Could be that I finally came to my senses. Or it could be that she has begun entertaining callers. So far, they've left a lot to be desired."

Just as he was about to grin and tell Lukas that he was glad he finally came to his senses, his buddy's words sank in. "What are you talking about? How can she already be receiving callers? She just got home from the hospital."

"Pierce Brenneman ain't wasting any time. He's been calling on her and being his normal, pushy self."

Simon didn't even try to hide his distaste. Pierce wasn't a bad sort, but he wasn't all that good, either. More importantly, Simon knew he wasn't a good fit for Amelia. She needed a man who was strong and able-bodied. Someone who could stand up to her overbearing brothers yet be gentle with her heart. Pierce was not that man. "You pushed me aside but are letting Pierce call on her? Can't say I'm real happy to hear that."

"He came by on his own. Actually, two times." Looking half amused, he added, "The first time he called, he told Amelia that he was glad they had goats in common."

"Goats? Honestly, Lukas."

"I know. I didn't know whether to laugh or give him a lesson on courting."

Simon didn't feel like laughing or giving tips. Instead, he was more concerned with Amelia's heart. "Who was home when he called the second time?"

"Darla. I haven't talked to her yet, but she stopped in to tell Rebecca today. She said Pierce was concerned about our family's routine."

"What routine?"

Lukas chuckled. "I said the same thing." He shrugged. "Darla and Rebecca seem to think Pierce is interested in using Amelia to become part of the family."

Using Amelia? That would be over his dead body.

Then, remembering all the ways Lukas had told him that he would never be good enough for Amelia, he said, "As fascinating as it is to hear about Amelia's love life, I don't understand why you are telling me about it."

"You know why."

"*Nee*. I do not."

Lukas sighed. "Because you and I and Rebecca and Darla and Amelia know you and Amelia were meant to be together."

"What changed? What happened to me not ever being able to remove my tattoos? What about needing to understand that I was never going to be good enough for your little sister?"

"I realized that I was being narrow-minded. My father had no patience for that. He would have been so angry with me for the way I treated you. Listen, I know it will take some time, but I'm hoping you will be able to forgive some of the other things I said, too. It was wrong for me to bring up your past. If you want to know the truth, I think in some ways I've been envious of you."

Simon raised his eyebrows. "Envious of being abused, taking drugs, breaking the law, and going to jail?"

"Envious of being brave enough to look beyond our community. I never did that. Not even during my *rumspringa*. Instead, I simply worked and planned to take my place here one day."

"You did everything right, Lukas. We've all been proud of you. You're the best man I know."

"I think my recent actions have proved that I have just as many faults as anyone else. Maybe even more."

Simon wanted to believe Lukas's words. But more than that, he didn't want be pushed away again. "I don't want my past to tarnish Amelia. And while I don't intend for it to, I really don't want you making me feel like I'm bad for her."

"You're not." Lukas stared hard at him. "Your past made you into the man you are. It's never bothered me. I've always thought you were a strong person and someone who I could depend on. I should have realized that it was going to make you someone special to Amelia, too."

"So, are you saying I can come calling on her?"

"*Jah*. But, well, just be careful with her heart, wouldja? If you decide she ain't the woman for you, try to let her down gently."

Simon knew that wasn't going to be the case. "I'll treat her with care." Just like he always had. "I'm coming over tonight, too. I could care less about your routine."

"Noted." He stepped back, then blurted, "I left Levi a message and asked him to come home."

Simon hadn't realized Lukas had known where Levi was. "What did he say?"

"I don't know. I left a message on the answering service at his work, but he hasn't returned my call yet."

"Where is he?"

"Florida. Working construction."

"Why did you contact him? For Amelia?"

"*Jah*. Plus, it was time. I've always understood his need for a break. I wasna exactly happy about it, but I understood. But I could use his help. It's too much."

"You've got Darla now."

"I do. I have her and her family and I don't want her to think I'm neglecting them."

"She knows how busy you are."

"She knows, but . . ." He shrugged.

"I understand."

Hearing the rumble of a truck approaching, Simon grabbed his clipboard. "Delivery's here, so I've got to go. I'll be seeing you tonight."

"Thanks, Simon. And I am sorry."

"No need to mention it," he said over his shoulder as he watched two men climb out of the truck. "It's in the past." And good riddance, too.

"Simon, is everything all right?" Trent asked when he got to his side.

"It will be if these guys got our order right for once."

That was all he could share. Because everything else was simply too good to share aloud.

Chapter 12

Friday, October 9

Amelia was far too old to spend much more time lazing about on the couch and watching the world go by out the living room window. It was now Friday, officially over a week since she'd had her accident.

During that time, she'd slept a lot. At first, she'd been in pain, too. But now she was feeling a bit better physically . . . but becoming increasingly restless.

She had always been the person to take care of their farm. She'd gardened and cooked, cleaned and laundered. Now all she could do was sit.

Shifting uncomfortably, Amelia watched Darla's sisters Maisie and Gretel play with Oscar outside. Over and over again, they tossed a stuffed squeaky toy a short distance. The motion was met with a happy yip and then little Oscar would lumber toward the toy, somehow pick it up with his under bite, and bring it to the girls.

It was a sweet scene. Even sweeter was seeing Darla's other siblings working in the yard. Samuel and Evan pulled weeds while Patsy gathered eggs and swept off the front porch. Just beyond them, Darla's brother Aaron had their two horses tied up to some posts and was giving them a good brushing and rubdown. His fiancée, Hope, was by his side, giving Princess attention. Now that things had settled down at the Kurtz house, the siblings seemed more relaxed and like their old selves.

All of these chores were things that Amelia did over the course of one day. It was slightly alarming to see so many hands doing them at one time. It also made her feel kind of good about herself. She knew she'd done a lot around the house and farm. Now perhaps the rest of the family realized it, too!

"How is everyone doing out there? Does anyone need better instruction?" Darla asked Amelia as she entered the living room with a tray loaded with soup, saltines, and a tall glass of apple juice.

"All any of them needs is my thanks." Smiling as she watched the small crowd work so industriously, Amelia added, "I think they are all doing a fine job. It's kind of them to come over to do so much work."

After setting the tray on the coffee table, Darla peeked out the window. "I promise, they were happy to help. Besides, the girls wanted to see the puppy, and Hope is almost as smitten with Princess as you are."

"Princess is a *gut* goat, for sure. But if Hope is smitten, Aaron should get her one."

Darla chuckled. "Ah, you can be the one to tell him that! They just set a wedding date, so I think they have enough on their plate."

"When is the wedding?"

"January sixth."

"A New Year's bride. A wonderful blessing."

"I think so," Darla said with a sweet smile. "After all the tragedies we've had in the last year, it will be wonderful to begin the year in a better way. I cannot wait to celebrate their union, too. Aaron and Hope have had to overcome so many challenges."

Amelia privately reflected that Darla had, too. About six months ago Darla had been overwhelmed and hurting. People in the community were blaming her father for the mill's fire, and her mother, unable to take the accusations and grief, had left the whole family. In addition, Aaron had been so angry that he was taking it out on her and her siblings. Darla had borne the weight of it all.

"Lots of us have been facing many challenges," Amelia pointed out quietly. "Lord knows that you've had your fair share."

Darla shrugged. "You're right. Most of us in Charm could say the same thing. If they weren't affected by the fire, they had other, more personal troubles to bear. But that's what life is, don't you think? A mixture of peaks and valleys and turns."

Darla's words made her think of Simon and his struggles. "Yet the road always goes forward," she murmured.

Darla's bright-blue eyes warmed. "Indeed. No matter how windy or convoluted our paths seem, we must all keep going. We've got no choice but to do that." She turned back to the window and smiled. "Uh-oh. I think Oscar has finally had his fill of all that attention. He looks like he's about to collapse. I'll go see if I can rescue him from my sisters."

Just moments after Darla walked out the front door, Amelia heard the faint complaints of Gretel and Maisie. She giggled to herself as she sipped her soup and munched on a couple of crackers.

Darla was right, and her words had served to be a good reminder. She needed to stop fretting about Amelia's love life. While it was obvious that Pierce was not the man for her, it didn't mean that he was the only option. If he was coming out of the woodwork, chances were good that someone else would, too. Sooner or later, the right man would appear in her life. She needed to adopt an open heart and mind and let that happen.

But as she heard more laughter outside the window, she realized that that was easier said than done. She missed her family and missed being in the thick of things. She wasn't going to whine or complain, though. Studiously, she concentrated on her soup and tried not to feel sorry for herself. Before long, she would be back on her feet and this moment would be just a memory.

It was too bad her soup now tasted like dishwater.

When the door opened, she put down her spoon. "Do you have Oscar?" she asked whoever had just entered. "If so, I can watch him. He likes to sit on the couch next to me."

"I don't have a bulldog. But if you want company, I could sit next to you," Simon said with a teasing smile. "That is, if you'd let me."

Amelia just about choked on her cracker. "What are you doing here?"

Against her will, she noticed that he'd freshly showered. The ends of his light-brown hair were damp. Even from across the room, he smelled fresh and clean. Like the yellow Dial soap he'd once told her he favored.

No man should ever look that handsome.

He hadn't moved. Staring at her from across the room, he

said, "There are a number of reasons why I came. But the most important is that I was concerned about how you were feeling."

She was having trouble understanding. "Concerned?"

"*Jah*. I wanted to check on you. Sorry it's taken me so long to get here."

He was apologizing for his delayed visit? *That's* what he was sorry for?

Intending to let him know how she felt, she said, "Simon, I don't know why you are apologizing. There is no need."

"Sure there is. We left things in a bad way."

She hated how he was rewriting their history. "*We* did not leave things in a bad way. *You* informed *me* that you shouldn't have been spending time with me. I didn't misunderstand a thing. It was real clear." And because she was so mad, she added something a bit mean. "Crystal clear."

Her jab hit its mark. A muscle jumped in his cheek. "Amelia, don't be like this," Simon cajoled. "You know why I said the things I did. I want what is best for you."

"You don't know what I want or need."

"I know I don't. But your brother and sister seemed to—"

"They seem to want to run my life," she interrupted. "Which you were happy to let them do without consulting me." When he flinched with a hurt expression, she inwardly groaned. She hated hurting his feelings. However, he'd certainly hurt hers.

As the awful tension between them worsened, she ached to leave the room. Ack, but she couldn't even believe that she was stuck on this couch! She would give anything to hop off and seek the solace of her room.

Simon, however, seemed to be of a very different mind. Look-

Ing more determined than ever, he said, "Amy, we need to talk about this in a calm way. Can I sit down?"

She saw where he was looking. He was ready to sit down right next to her. "Not on this couch," she blurted. If he was too close, she was going to weaken like she always did around him. In order to stand firm, she was going to need a good amount of space between them. As much as possible.

"Fair enough." He walked right over to the brown leather recliner in front of her and sat. "Now, may we talk about what happened?"

She wanted to, but if she let him in she knew what would happen. He would apologize and smile at her in a way that made her think of things she shouldn't. Her heart—along with her insides—would melt. Then, before she knew it, she would be agreeing to whatever he wanted. Because that was what she always did: She agreed to what Simon wanted because she wanted him more than she wanted what was right.

Amelia had had a lot of time to think about things over the last few days, and she'd come to the conclusion that her judgment was flawed—where he was concerned, anyway. She'd pushed aside her sister's warnings about Simon's history. She'd ignored the rumors she'd heard about him keeping company with dangerous people. She'd pretended she'd never heard her father whispering about writing to Simon in jail.

More recently, she'd kept Simon's visits a secret from her sister and brother. And yet when his visits had come to light, after she'd defended their relationship, he'd given her up as if she wasn't all that important to him after all.

She'd waited for him to come to his senses and hurry to her side and apologize, but he hadn't. Not for days.

She'd cried over him. She'd listened to far too many lectures from her sister about how there were other men in the world who would treat her far better. Now she almost believed that.

If she went back now, that would make her an even bigger fool than she was already.

"Simon, we can talk, but I don't think there's much you can say that I will want to hear."

He nodded. "That's fair enough." After staring at her for a moment, he said, "Amelia, you were right. I shouldn't have let your brother's words sway me. I should have talked to you about what he said and about how I feel, too."

"That would have been helpful."

"Amelia, I am sorry. I let my doubts and worries that I'll never be good enough for you interfere with everything I knew was right." Still staring at her intently, he lowered his voice. "I should have believed in us as much as you do."

Yes, he should have.

Ack! *Nee.* As much as she *used* to believe in them! She had already moved on.

Well, kind of.

Leaning forward, Simon rested his elbows on his knees. His hazel eyes were cloudy with concern. He looked tense, too.

Feeling her determination to shield herself from him fade, she asked helplessly, "What did Lukas say to you? What did he say that made you change your mind?"

"He reminded me that I couldn't change my past. That it would always be with me."

"And why did this matter?"

A line formed between his brows. "What do you mean?"

"You had already told me a lot of things that you had done.

I knew they weren't good. I also knew that you had done some things that you never wanted to share. I respected that."

He nodded slowly. "But I can never completely escape my past. That means . . . well, that means if you were mine, you'd have to deal with my past, too."

If she were his. Down went her guard just a little more. "If not me, then who?"

"Pardon?"

"If not me, then who? Who would be the right girl for you?"

He straightened, his hands coming to brace himself on the couch. "Amelia, you can't ask me that."

"Why not?"

"Because I don't know who else would be the right girl."

"Because?"

He stared at her intently. "Because I only want you."

Oh, but those were the words that her dreams had been made of. She was almost afraid to look at her feet, because she was fairly certain that the last of her defenses were now lying in a forgotten heap on the ground.

With effort, she made herself remember crying over him in the empty hospital room. "You only want me *now, jah*?"

"No. I've only wanted you *ever*. I was simply trying to do the right thing." Looking embarrassed, he said, "I was weak. I started dreading how you would look at me when you learned more about my past."

"Ever since my *mamm* died so long ago, I have tried my best to be one of those people who deals with the present and the future. Not fixating on how things might have been different." Carefully, she continued. "But in this instance, in relation to you and me . . . I think that habit is wrong."

"What are you saying?"

She was shaking inside. "Simon, I want to know everything about you. I want to know the things you've done that you don't want me to know about. The things that you've never even shared with Lukas or Levi."

He visibly paled. "I can't do that."

"Why not?"

"Because I don't want you to know, Amelia. I promise, you don't want to know all the things I've done."

"Simon, if you want me, then I want all of you. *All of you*," she repeated.

"I can't . . . I can't give you that."

He was still keeping her at a distance. Still.

Feeling disappointed, both for his walls and her inability to see that they'd never be the couple she dreamed of, Amelia knew it was time to let him go.

Feeling like a weight was pressing on her chest, she said, "If you can't give me all of you, then I guess you better leave and go in search of the right woman." She hoped she would actually be able to survive if he did just that.

Hurt filled his gaze. "You're really going to send me away? While you stay and let that . . . that Pierce come calling on you?"

"Pierce ain't the man for me. But like you said, there are others."

Slowly, he got to his feet. "I didn't say there were others. I said there was only you."

She turned her head away. If she looked his way, he'd see her tears. He'd know how much she was hurting. He'd know that she really did love him.

She felt him standing motionless in front of her. Simply staring at her. She kept her head turned away and fixated firmly on her clenched fists.

A full minute later, he turned and left.

Only then did she let the tears fall. She'd not only hurt herself, but she'd hurt him, too.

He'd come here full of sweet words and hope. He'd been sure that she would trust him. That she would want him, no matter what.

Instead, she'd wounded his spirit.

Funny, but she would rather have gotten kicked by a goat and bitten by a snake again than to realize she was capable of causing so much pain.

Chapter 13

Saturday, October 10

It was a quarter after nine in the evening and Rebecca, Jacob, Lukas, and Darla had been attempting to quit playing cards for the last half hour. It wasn't going so well. The moment one of them made a move to stand up, someone else would make a comment or a joke. The next thing they knew, another ten minutes had passed.

Lukas didn't mind their late night, though. Between the demands at work and the needs of his and Darla's families, he was rarely able to take time to simply play cards and laugh. Their evening had been good medicine.

"So, are we gonna play another round of hearts or call it a night?"

"We need to call it a night," Rebecca said as she started shuffling the cards.

Lukas couldn't help but smile at that. It looked like his sister had been needing this carefree evening together as much as he had.

Glancing at the clock, Jacob raised his brows. "If we're not careful, it's going to be a quarter after ten before we know it."

Darla glanced his way and grinned. "Probably. The last time I looked at the clock, it was a little after seven."

His wife had a point. Time did fly when the four of them were together. Lukas had been surprised—though, he knew he shouldn't have been—that he, his sister, and their spouses had taken to doing "couple things" so easily. But it still came as a bit of a shock.

Ever since their father had passed away, he and Becky had been overwhelmed with responsibility. Levi's need for a break hadn't helped things. Amelia had managed things at home, but though he appreciated her help with supper and laundry, those efforts hadn't alleviated the constant weight of responsibility he felt at the mill.

Just weeks after the fire, Rebecca had looked at him sadly and said that they were sure to be in for lots of rocky days while they adjusted to their new realities.

She had not been wrong.

But what neither she nor he had anticipated was that they also seemed to be thriving. They had both married. Jacob was a good, calm counterpart for Rebecca and a welcome addition to the mill. And Darla? Well, she'd always been one of his best friends. Now they were closer than ever—and happier than they'd ever been.

These were unexpected blessings, for sure and for certain.

Leaning over, Jacob gently pulled the playing cards from his wife's hands. "It really is time for us to be getting home, Rebecca. Church is tomorrow, and it's going to be at least a forty-minute buggy ride."

"You're right."

"We're going with my parents, too, you know. That means we'll be getting up extra early so we won't be late."

With a sigh, Rebecca stood up. "They do like to be places on time." Just as Jacob was about to help her with her cloak, she looked at Lukas. "Do you think Amelia is going to be all right? She went to bed awfully early. She didn't want to join us for cards, either."

Lukas didn't know the answer to that. Unable to help himself, he looked down the hall yet again. "I don't know."

"I'm thinking she was simply tired," Darla said. "I sat with her before you came over. She says she has a hard time sleeping since she isn't doing much activity."

"Plus, she's lugging around a heavy cast," Jacob added. "That can't be easy."

Rebecca worried her bottom lip but nodded. "I hadn't thought about that."

Lukas cleared his throat. "I promise that Darla and I will look after Amelia tomorrow. Don't worry about her."

"I'm just thinking that maybe there's a lot more on her mind than her accident. I know she's still upset about Simon." Turning to her sister-in-law, she said, "Are you sure you didn't accidentally overhear anything when he came over?"

"I'm sure." Holding up a hand, she said wryly, "I didn't hear a thing accidentally or on purpose."

"Did you even try to listen?"

After looking at Lukas, Darla shook her head. *"Nee."*

"She deserves her privacy, Beck," Lukas said. He still felt guilty that he'd interfered in her life so much.

But Rebecca didn't look like she agreed completely. "Giving

Simon and Amelia privacy is all well and good, but it's also un-helpful. If we don't know what is going on, how are we supposed to find out how to help them?"

Jacob chuckled. "Settle down, Beck."

She squirmed. "I'm settled. Kind of. But this is important."

"I don't think she wants our help now," Darla interjected smoothly. "I don't know how Lukas feels, but I have to say that I am not in any hurry to interfere, either."

"I'm not saying another word to either of them about their relationship," Lukas vowed.

"Oh, Lukas. Don't be like that."

He barely refrained from shaking his head in frustration. They were older, they were married, but it was obvious that some things never changed. Once again Rebecca was determined to fix everything as quickly as possible. "Don't be like what? Patient?" he prodded. "I happen to learn from my mistakes. You should try to do that, too."

"Don't act so smug. I have learned something. And that is why I want to try to help in some way."

Jacob rested a hand on her arm. "I'm afraid I agree with Lukas. We'll talk to Amelia when she is ready. Until then, we will honor her wishes to keep her conversations private."

Relieved that Jacob was on his side, Lukas nodded. "Our in-terference didn't do any of them any favors, Becky."

"We won't be interfering if we know they are the perfect match." Looking up at Jacob fondly, she added, "Just like we are."

Lukas groaned. "If you are going to start saying gushy things like that, it's time to walk you out the door."

Jacob laughed. "I agree. Not because I don't like Rebecca's

pretty words, but because I fear she's after one thing only—for me to tell her that she's right."

"I'm not that bad," she protested.

"Yes, you are," Lukas said. "But since we're used to your ways, we'll still keep you around."

Grinning up at him, Rebecca said softly, "You're going to keep me around because you love me?"

"*Jah,* because of that. But mainly because you are the only person who can keep everything straight at work. I can't risk you getting mad at me," he teased.

Rebecca looked stunned. "I think you mean that!"

"I know he does," Darla quipped. "My husband might not sing your praises to your face, but he certainly sings them when you aren't around."

"That's good to hear," she said with a little lift of her chin. "It's always good to feel needed."

Jacob wrapped an arm around Rebecca's shoulders. "*Gut.* Because I need you to let me get home."

Lukas stood at the window until he saw the light on the back of their buggy fade into the distance. When Darla came to stand next to him, he asked softly, "Want me to help you clean up?"

"*Nee.* There's not much to worry about. I'll do the rest of the dishes in the morning." She shifted and wrapped her arms around his middle, linking her hands together. "I'd rather stand like this for a little bit longer."

He couldn't deny that the feel of her in his arms was comforting. It always had been. "Do you think we're making the right decision with Amelia? Maybe Rebecca is right."

"She isn't. She's happy, so she wants everyone around her to be happy, too. But you and I know it ain't that easy. Everyone has their own path to take. Sometimes it's best to simply get out of their way."

Bending down, he kissed her temple. "You are so smart. That's probably why I married you."

As he'd hoped, she laughed. "And here I thought it was because of my other charms."

Thinking of those charms, he moved from the window. "Are you terribly tired, Darla?"

Those blue eyes that he loved so much gleamed. "Never that tired."

As he turned off the kerosene lantern and followed his wife up the stairs to their bedroom, he couldn't help but smile. Yes, things were busy and work was demanding, but there were other things in his life that were terribly sweet.

Chapter 14

Monday, October 12

Amelia was doing that thing she did with her nose when she was annoyed. From the time she was four or five, she'd wrinkled her nose whenever her siblings did something she didn't like. They'd all thought it was kind of cute when she was small. Levi and Rebecca had teased her mercilessly about it when she was a teen.

Now? Lukas took it in stride. "Your nose is gonna stay that way if you ain't careful, sister."

Instantly, she smoothed her expression. "Honestly, Lukas," she said around a dramatic sigh. "I wish you hadn't come home from work early."

"That ain't any way to greet your brother," he teased as he handed her a cup of hot tea liberally laced with honey before sitting down on the coffee table in front of her. "You're going to hurt my feelings."

Her nose wrinkled again. "Oh, stop. And get up off that table. You're going to break it if you're not careful."

He doubted that, but he moved to his father's old easy chair next to the fireplace. "You don't seem very chipper today. What's wrong?"

"What's wrong is that you're here. I told you this morning, there was no reason on earth for you to come home from the mill early." She waved a hand. "Yet, here you are."

He would have smiled if he didn't think she was about to lose her last bit of composure. "For your information, there is absolutely a reason for me to have come home. It's a *gut* one, too."

A spark of interest appeared in her eyes. "Oh? What is it?"

"You."

"I can get to the kitchen and bathroom just fine on my own now," she grumbled.

"There are other things I could do around here besides help you up and down the halls."

"Like what?" she asked peevishly. "I can't see you doing much good with the laundry."

Never again would he take her even temper for granted! "Settle down, little sister. You're beginning to sound like a fishwife."

Amelia drew in a breath, obviously ready to argue that, too . . . then she blew out a sigh. "I know. I'm sorry."

"You don't need to be sorry. Instead, accept help when it is offered. You have given me a good reason to take a break from work. Plus, Darla wouldn't have left to go to the post office if that meant you were home alone." He glared for good measure. "Everything ain't all about you, you know."

"I know." To his shock, tears appeared in her eyes. "I'm so

sorry. You are right." Plucking at the quilt on her lap, she said, "I'm just not used to being so inactive. I hate sitting around, especially when there is so much to do. It's making me peevish."

"I noticed." He was just about to remind her that she'd be up on her feet in no time when they heard a knock at the door. "You expecting anyone?" he asked as he stood up.

For some reason, that question made her look even more depressed. *"Nee."*

"I bet it's some ladies bringing by another casserole. I'll be right back." He opened the door, fully intending to politely thank whomever had just arrived before eventually storing the dish in the freezer. Their neighbors had been so generous, he, Darla, and Amelia couldn't eat everything right away.

Except it wasn't a lady. It was a man about his age. He was tall, as tall as himself, wearing a black coat over a white shirt and black trousers. Thick work boots covered his feet.

"May I help you?"

"Jah. This is the Kinsinger *haus, jah?"*

Lukas nodded. "Are you needing something?" Maybe he was trying to apply for a job? Every once in a while someone came to the house instead of the mill to approach him about work.

"I think so. Are you Lukas Kinsinger?"

"I am."

"I'm Benjamin Miller."

"Hi." In a firm tone, he said, "Listen, if you are looking for work, you made a mistake. You need to go to the mill and apply. This is my home."

"Oh, I'm not here for work." He stuck out a hand. "Like I said, my name is Benjamin Miller. Ben to everyone who knows me. I met you and your father at a charity auction a year ago."

Lukas shook the man's hand. He didn't remember meeting him, but if he had been with his father, he likely hadn't been paying much attention to men his *daed* talked to. Slightly annoyed that the guy had shown up unannounced, Lukas said, "I'm sorry to tell you this, but my father ain't here. He, uh, passed away."

"I know that." Ben pulled off his black felt hat. "I'm real sorry about your loss, Lukas. I didn't know him real well, of course, but he was real respected. He was a *gut* man."

"He was." Shaking off the momentary sadness that consumed him every time he thought about his father, Lukas eyed the visitor closely. "I'm sorry, but I still don't understand why you are here."

His cheeks flushed. "Oh. Sorry. I'm here for Amelia."

This whole episode was getting stranger and stranger. Lukas gripped the side of the door. "Say again?"

"I'm here for Amelia. You know. Your sister." The corners of his lips tilted up at the corners. "I met her at the auction, too."

"Over a year ago."

"*Jah.* My cousin works at the hospital. She told me that Amelia Kinsinger spent a day there a week ago. I guess she got herself a broken leg?"

"I wouldn't say she got it on her own. A goat had something to do with it."

Ben laughed. "Goats have sturdy hooves. Ain't so?"

"Uh-huh."

"When I heard she was injured, I decided to pay a call on her."

"I didn't realize you two were close." In fact, Lukas was pretty sure this Ben was definitely *not* close to his sister.

"We're not. But a man can hope." He smiled in a winsome way. "I'm real glad you're here and not at the mill today."

"Because?"

"Because I'm here to ask permission to call on her."

Lukas barely stopped himself from wrinkling his own nose. "This seems rather out of the blue."

"Maybe to you. But I've been thinking about her for some time. She was so sweet when we met."

Lukas knew the man was likely remembering her looks. Honestly, he was tempted to simply shut the door in Ben's face. What kind of a man was he? He had a lot of nerve, calling on Amelia uninvited, all because he'd heard some story about her being in the hospital. "I don't know how I can give permission," he replied, making sure that his tone conveyed his displeasure with Ben. "I don't know you."

"My family are third-generation farmers. We have a two-hundred-acre place right north of Millersburg. We've invested in the area, too. Furthermore, my uncle is Amos Miller. He was good friends with your *daed*."

Lukas swallowed. Now it was all coming back. His father had been happy to talk to Amos and had been cordial to this Benjamin, too. He'd even whispered to Lukas that they were a well-respected family. In short, this man was everything that his father would have probably wanted for Amelia.

It was too bad Lukas didn't think very highly of him. But after he'd done so much wrong with Simon, he was afraid to interfere again.

"Amelia doesn't need my permission," he said at last. "She is choosing her own suitors."

Benjamin's eyes lit up. "That's *gut*."

"*Jah*. It's great." Feeling like he was letting in a tax collector, he waved a hand. "You might as well come on in."

"Danke."

After Benjamin stepped through the doorway looking delighted, Lukas said, "Let me go tell my sister you are here. It will be up to her to decide if she feels like talking to you. There's a good chance she won't." He really hoped not.

In one blink, that ridiculous grin vanished. "Huh."

Huh, indeed. Lukas found himself practically stalking down the hallway.

Amelia looked up from the magazine she was flipping through. "Who was at the door?"

"Benjamin Miller from Millersburg."

She shrugged. "I don't know him. Do you work with Benjamin?"

"*Nee*. He is here for you."

She sat up a little straighter. "Really? Why?"

"It seems you, me, and Daed met him at a charity auction about a year ago. I remember it vaguely. Maybe. Daed knew his uncle."

After tossing the magazine on the coffee table, she shifted and smoothed out the pink dress and white apron she had on. "Daed liked this man?"

"I wouldn't say that. Daed knew him, which isn't that noteworthy. Daed knew pretty much everyone in two counties."

"I suppose he did."

Grudgingly, he added, "I might remember Daed saying that his family is a good one. Respected."

"Ah."

Feeling better now that he saw that Amelia wasn't all that excited about having an unannounced caller either, he asked, "What do you want me to do with this Benjamin? He seems to think you might allow him to call on you." Unable to not sound hopeful, he asked, "Would you like me to send him away?"

"Of course not. I'd be happy to see him."

"You would?"

"Why wouldn't I? I need to start courting, and it's not like I can go out to frolic or anything."

He supposed she had a point. But that didn't mean he wanted her sitting alone with a stranger. "How about I bring him in and join you?"

"Like a chaperone?" She wrinkled her nose.

"Not 'like.' I would be your chaperone."

"That won't be necessary, *bruder,*" she said, her tone firm. "You may bring him down the hall. And then you can go do something else."

Everything inside of him wanted to protest. To remind her that she was still a young, innocent girl and this caller was altogether too forward. But he'd promised himself to never interfere again.

"Fine. But I'm going to be in the kitchen just in case you need me."

"*Danke,* Lukas."

He turned on his heel and walked back down the hall.

Ben was standing awkwardly in the foyer. When he spied Lukas, he smiled. "What did she say?"

"You may follow me. Amelia said you can visit with her for fifteen minutes."

"That's all?"

"That's more time than I would have given you. Come on." When he arrived back in the hearth room, he performed the necessary introductions. "Amelia, this is Benjamin Miller. Ben, my sister Amelia. I'll be back in fifteen minutes."

"Hello, Ben. Won't you sit down?"

Lukas turned on his heel before he heard any more. When he finally arrived in the comfort of the kitchen, he braced his hands on the sink and released a ragged breath. "I hope you are happy, God," he said. "I know you were exactly right. It was much better for Amy to be seeing Simon than this fool. Or that . . . that Pierce, even. But just to let you know, I have no need for anymore reminders. I'm going to find a way to get Amelia and Simon back together. It needs to happen soon. The sooner the better."

Then he sat down on a kitchen chair and watched the clock until it was time to get Ben Miller out of his house.

Chapter 15

Wednesday, October 14

Simon wouldn't say that walking back up the Kinsingers' long driveway was one of the hardest things he'd ever done, but it surely felt like it was among the most important.

Last night he'd worked on his farm. He'd trimmed bushes and pruned trees and weeded the flower beds. Later, he'd walked out to the barn and swept the cement floor and tried to envision it not as a place for animals but as a refuge for kids. He began to mentally remove horse stalls and replace them with chairs and couches. Someplace where teenagers would be able to relax for a few hours at a time.

And the more he looked around, the more he realized that his seed of an idea might bear fruit after all. It wouldn't be hard to convert the old barn to the haven he was imagining. More importantly, he had come to realize that the project wasn't only going to be good for kids, but good for his soul, too.

When he'd walked back inside to clean up the last of his

supper dishes, he thought about Tess's visit a few nights ago. Finally, he was coming to believe that she was right. He wasn't perfect. He was actually very far from that. However, the Lord didn't expect or want him to be perfect.

Instead, the Lord wanted Simon to follow his heart. And that heart not only belonged to Tess and his friends . . . it was firmly in Amelia's keeping.

He adored Amelia. He wanted her heart, too, and he knew his intentions for her were true. He wanted to court her with consideration. Take care of her. Be everything she needed. And he knew he could be, too. Because he knew no one would ever love her like he did.

Just before he'd gotten into bed, he remembered something else Tess had told him.

"I'm proud of you," she'd said. "*Nee,* that's not right. I'm proud of both of us."

"You think we deserve to feel that way?"

"Oh, yes," she'd said. "We may be scarred and marked and a little bit damaged, but we're not throwaway people, Simon. We have worth."

Her words had given him pause. "You really think so?"

"I know it. We're just as good as anyone." Looking at him pointedly, she said, "Even your Amelia."

"I hope you're right."

"I know I am. Because I love you."

"I, ah, I love you, too."

"*Gut.* If you love Amelia as much as you say you do, go out and visit her again. Keep trying and don't give up."

Those words had reverberated in his head all night long.

Now, as he walked to her house, Simon reflected on everything he'd done wrong with both Amelia and Lukas. Since his mistakes couldn't be undone, he knew it was time to stop dwelling on them.

Instead, he needed to be honest and open. Amelia needed to know that he was in love with her and that he was willing to do whatever it took to return to her good graces.

Time wasn't an issue. If it took him two days, two weeks, or two months, he was willing to be patient. But he hoped it wouldn't take two years.

Just as he was walking up the front walkway to the Kinsingers' home, Darla opened the front door. "Hi, Simon."

"Hey." Though he'd known her almost as long as Lukas had, it still took him off guard to see how petite she was. Maybe it was because she had a rather assertive personality. When they were in school, she'd excelled at bossing everyone around. But now she looked so calm and peaceful; it was obvious that her marriage to Lukas was agreeing with her. She looked pretty in a forest-green dress. It set off her auburn hair and blue eyes.

"I'm glad to see you here."

"Really? How are things?" Of course, as soon as he asked that question, he wished he'd had the nerve to ask about Amelia.

Studying him carefully, she said, "I'm not sure at the moment."

He drew to a stop. "Not sure what that means, Darla. Is something wrong with Amelia?"

"I hope not."

"Darla, talk to me." He could practically feel his blood pressure rising. Was Amelia hurting? Had she gotten an infection? He'd overheard the nurses telling her that was a possibility.

After taking a quick glance behind her, Darla stepped farther out onto the porch and closed the door. "I was washing a couple of

Oscar's paw prints from the windowsill when I noticed you through the glass. I guess you're calling on Amelia all proper-like now?"

"I am." He couldn't help that his voice was guarded. Finally, having the chance to call on Amelia publicly meant too much to him.

"Good luck with that." She didn't sound sarcastic . . . but she didn't sound all that hopeful, either.

Even though Darla's opinion didn't really matter to him one way or another, he decided to get things out in the open. "I might as well know. Are you for me and Amelia becoming a couple or not?"

"I'm for it, of course."

"Of course?" He didn't even try to conceal his amazement.

"Well, *jah*. To be sure," she said with a puzzled smile. "You are a grown man who had to be a grown-up even when you were young. And while I don't know everything about your past, I don't need to know it, either."

"That's not what Lukas thought."

She shrugged. "Lukas is my husband, but that doesn't mean we have to agree on absolutely everything. Especially not matters of the heart. All that matters to me is one simple thing."

"What is that?"

"That ever since I've known you, you've had a soft spot for Amelia." Her blue eyes twinkled. "Even when we all were in school together."

Embarrassed, he winced. "I didn't realize I had been that obvious."

"You weren't. Lukas didn't notice you pining, of course, but that don't mean much. He's always had the mill on his mind."

"And you, from time to time."

She grinned. "*Jah*. And me from time to time, too." She shrugged. "Anyway, after everything we've all been through, the last thing I'd ever want to do is interfere with anyone's hope of happiness."

"I appreciate that." Tired of waiting, he stepped toward the door. "So, may I go on in?"

"You may. Amelia's in the back hearth room. But I think I should warn you that she's probably not going to greet you with the same enthusiasm that I did."

"I'm not expecting her to." Just before he turned the knob, he thought of something new. "Darla, is Amelia still worried about Lukas and Rebecca giving their blessings?"

"Oh, *nee*. She's moved on from that."

She looked like she was about to burst out laughing while he felt ready to pull his hair out. "Do you mind telling me what has got you so amused?"

"Only that she's been fairly snippy with all of us. Mighty un-Amelia-like. She's pretty much told everyone to stop interfering."

"Those feelings might be justified," he said before realizing that he was as much to blame as her siblings.

Practically reading his mind, she said, "I don't think she's real thrilled that you decided to leave the house the other day instead of sharing your past."

"I've got a lot of explaining to do."

"Maybe so."

"I'll do that, then. I have to. I can't stay away. But if my past upsets her, please know that I kept it from her for a reason."

"I understand." Lowering her voice, she said, "For what it's worth, I had to tell Lukas quite a few things about what had been going on in my house that were hard to share."

"Are you glad you did?"

She nodded.

Thinking of how Tess had reminded them they were worthy of love and friendship, he said slowly, "I'll try to do the same thing, then."

"Do you think you're going to be able to do that?" she asked gently.

"I can try. Otherwise, I'll regret it for the rest of my life." He had far too many regrets already.

She nodded. "Good to hear, but, uh, just in case you haven't heard . . . she's had a caller."

He turned to face her directly. "I know about Pierce."

"This is another one. Benjamin Miller."

Honestly, the moment his back was turned, men started coming out of the woodwork! "Who is he?"

"He lives over in Millersburg."

"Millersburg ain't all that close. How does he know Amelia?"

"They met at a charity auction or some such a year ago." Folding her arms over her chest, she smiled. "I thought you might find that noteworthy."

"She doesn't like him, does she?"

"I don't think so. She hardly knows him. But he's right fond of her. At least Lukas thought he seemed that way on Monday when he stopped by."

"I would have thought Lukas would be monitoring these visits better."

"I think Lukas might be a little wary about interfering. And I think the only reason Amelia even saw him was to make a point to her brother. If I were you, I'd tread carefully."

"I'll do my best," he said before he opened the door and went inside. As he walked down the short hallway, past the main living area and around the kitchen, Simon couldn't begin to count the number of times he'd followed this same path. He'd come over to see Lukas and Levi almost every day when he was little and at least once a week before he finally left.

The house was full of warm memories for him. Security, too. No matter how bad he looked or how down he might have been, the Kinsinger family had treated him as if he was a valued guest.

Never before had he experienced the trepidation he was feeling as he went in search of the one girl who'd always had his heart.

Amelia didn't know it, but he was only fragile around one person in the world and that was her. She had the power to crush him. It was really too bad he hadn't weighed the consequences of his actions before he'd told her that he couldn't see her anymore.

He walked quietly, half afraid he was going to wake her up. Half afraid that he'd have to immediately face her piercing blue eyes glaring at him like he was an interloper.

Sure enough, turning the corner, he was caught in her gaze. And because he was a master at pretending he was far more composed and cool than he was, he simply nodded his head. "You're awake. Good."

She blinked. "That is all you have to say to me?"

"Of course not," he said as he circled around the end of the couch and sat down on the cushioned ottoman so he could face her directly. "I've got a lot to say to you. The question is, are you ready to listen?"

Those pretty eyes of hers narrowed. "Simon Hochstetler, you have a lot of nerve coming over like this, full of attitude."

"And you have a lot of nerve letting every man in the county come wandering in to take your pulse."

"I am hardly doing that."

He leaned forward, resting his elbows on his knees. "Darla told me some man named Benjamin stopped by on Monday."

She looked away. "He was respectful. Polite, too."

"I bet he was." Simon didn't even try to hide the derision in his voice.

"What is that supposed to mean?"

He almost didn't tell her what he was really thinking. Almost. But because she meant more to him than anything, he knew he owed her more than mere words. He owed her the truth. "It means that I bet he sees you—and all that you are—and combines it with the Kinsinger name, and is willing to do just about anything to gain your acceptance. The fact that you were willing to give him any time at all is amazing. The fact that you gave him your smile and acceptance so easily? It's a miracle."

She frowned. "He seems to like me."

Seems? Her insecurity broke his heart. How could someone who looked like her, who was from a family like hers, have even an ounce of doubt about herself? "Of course he likes you. You're Amelia Kinsinger. You're *you*. What isn't there to like?"

She opened her mouth, shut it as if she was suddenly at a loss for words, then grimaced as she shifted positions.

Immediately, he threw away his argumentative stance. What was he doing, chewing on her about so many things that didn't matter when she had just been released from the hospital? He lowered his voice as he leaned down closer to her. "Are you in pain? Do you need something?"

"*Nee.*"

"Water?" Remembering her fondness for hot chocolate, he said, "How about some hot cocoa?"

"It's bright and sunny out, Simon."

He wasn't sure what that signified. "Does that mean you don't want any?"

"You would be correct." Rearranging herself again with a small grunt, she turned her head. "Let's talk about something else."

Switching places, he took a seat in the comfortable chair next to her. As he realized that she wasn't kicking him out, he relaxed. This was why he'd come to see her. So they could spend time together and so she'd learn to trust him again. "Name it," he said.

Then he braced himself for whatever was about to come next.

Chapter 16

At first Simon thought his heart was pounding so hard, it was beating in his ears. Then he realized the sound was coming from the Kinsingers' beautiful grandfather clock ticking in the hallway. It was the only sound that could be heard while he waited for Amelia to speak.

Still attempting to look far less rattled than he was, Simon leaned back in the comfortable leather chair and propped one foot on an opposite knee.

"Simon, tell me about Tess and Jeremy," Amelia said softly.

And just like that, the last of his composure slipped away. Even hearing his siblings' names caught him off guard. "My brother and sister?" he asked slowly. "Like I told you earlier, Tess is a pharmaceutical rep. She lives north of Columbus but is going to be in this area more often because her boss gave her a new territory." He cleared his throat. "As for Jeremy, well, I haven't seen him in over a decade. Not since he left our house."

"Tess hasn't seen him, either?"

"*Nee,* she did." Hating how much it hurt, he made himself continue. He had to do this for Amelia. "The last time she saw him, he was hanging around a bad crowd and doing things he shouldn't."

"Are you talking about him drinking or doing drugs?"

"*Jah*. He was doing drugs." He shifted in a weak attempt to make his body relax. "I don't want to sound harsh, but he's most likely out of my life for good."

"Poor Jeremy. I don't remember him real well, but I do remember him being really tall and liking chocolate."

"He was tall. And he did like chocolate," he said with some surprise. He hadn't thought about that in years.

"He was always nice to me." Her bottom lip trembled, but she held her composure. "Simon, I don't remember you ever mentioning them during any of your visits."

"That's because there wasn't much to talk about. They both left when I was only eleven or so."

"So you weren't close to them? Not ever?"

"I was."

That had been the problem, of course. He'd been too close to them. He'd depended on both of them to shield him from the worst things that happened in their house. When he was a little boy, they had. But after they left, he'd realized they could only take so much. Their father had made sure of that. Growing up in that house had instilled a need to take care of oneself first. To do anything else had been risky.

"Why haven't you tried to keep in contact with them?"

"Staying in touch is something both people have to want. I couldn't stay in contact with two people who didn't want me. I had no idea where they were. I only reconnected with Tess by accident."

"I'm so sorry. I remember when I was a little girl, Lukas always liked you to come over here, but he never said why." She flushed. "And I never asked."

"You were a little girl and I wouldn't have told you the truth even if you had asked me."

"Because it was easier to keep it to yourself?"

"Because it was easier to pretend it wasn't happening."

Her gaze turned soft. True compassion shown there. That compassion, that care, that acceptance was why Simon had gone against Rebecca and Lukas's wishes and pursued her. Receiving such compassion was as tempting to him as liquor to an alcoholic. Yet, unlike a bottle of gin, he couldn't imagine any ill side effects of being near her. She was everything he'd ever wanted.

"How did you end up in prison?"

He was so relieved she wasn't asking more about his family, he said lightly, "I told you. I was foolish and stupid."

"And taking drugs."

He jerked his head into a semblance of a nod. "Some. But I canna even blame that on the drugs. I simply made some bad choices and ended up paying for them."

When she continued to stare at him, it took everything he had to meet her gaze. "What was it like?"

He pretended he didn't understand. "What was *what* like?"

"Prison."

Now she needed details? "I don't like to talk about prison with anyone. I really don't want to talk about this with you."

"Because?"

"Because it was bad, Amy. It was hard and boring and scary, too. All that you need to know is that I was in, but I got out and I don't intend to ever go back."

"Well, I don't want to simply talk about goats and my leg and the weather. I want to know you. The real you."

"I'm afraid you won't like the real man you might find."

"I am fairly sure that I already know him." Her voice hard, she said, "Come now, Simon. Please, trust me. Tell me about things that matter."

She was right. He needed to do this. "Okay," he said slowly. "Prison was difficult. It was, um, about how you would expect." When she simply stared, he gave her what she wanted. "All right, fine. There were bars everywhere. They were white and they seemed to always either be peeling or freshly painted. The walls were gray and continually marked with dirty fingerprints and who knows what. It smelled like sweat and cigarettes and bleach. And it was filled with men who were broken and guards who had no shame. It was noisy and bright and the days were endless and the nights worse."

"Did you have a roommate?"

She looked so hopeful, he almost covered his face to hide his look of dismay. "Um, not at first. But then I did."

She bit her lip. "Did you get along?"

"Amelia, we were in prison, honey. No one made friends."

"You look upset. Did . . . did he hurt you?"

"*Nee*. He was just a scared kid. And I . . . well, I was fairly angry and mean then. Not too many men wanted to mess with me."

She seemed to process that for a moment. "People have talked about you, you know."

"I bet they have."

Pointing to the sleeves of his shirt, she said, "Are you ever going to show me your tattoo?"

"Jah." Figuring he might as well get it over with, he said, "There's more than one. I've got several."

Amelia was looking at his arms as if trying real hard to imagine what they looked like. He didn't blame her; he would have done the same thing.

"Show me," she said at last.

Here it was. Exactly what Lukas said would happen, and exactly what he'd mistakenly pretended he didn't care about. Feeling as if he was about to expose far more of himself than he was ready for, he slowly unbuttoned one of his shirt cuffs and rolled it up.

She watched intently. He could almost feel her examining each inch of skin as it was revealed. Little by little, the first band of barbed wire became visible.

Then the next.

Finally, the third.

Because he tried to keep them covered up when he was around others, his skin was pale, making the black ink stand out even more than it would have otherwise.

When his shirtsleeve was rolled up as far as it could go, which was just before the bulge of his bicep, he stretched out his left arm and moved it a bit so she could see all the bands, as well as the intricate design on his forearm in blue and red.

She leaned forward. Then, to his surprise, she reached out and carefully traced one of the bands. "It looks so dark, I thought it might be raised."

Was that all she had to say? *"Nee.* My skin is smooth."

"Are there more?"

"Jah."

"More bands?"

"*Jah*. And some writing. And . . . and a mark from the prison."
He pointed to his right shoulder blade. "That was my first. I've
got twelve in all."

"Twelve. Did they hurt, Simon?"

"*Jah.*" Some hurt more than others. Some not enough. He'd
stopped marking himself when he'd realized that he hadn't enjoyed the tattoos themselves as much as the process of getting
them. He'd realized then that he'd wanted to feel the sharp
pinch of the needles. Then he could remember that he was still
capable of feeling . . . that he hadn't become completely numb.

"Can I see the others, too?"

"Since I'd have to take off my shirt to show you, no." He
smiled then. "Darla would toss me out and I'd never get to
return."

To his surprise, Amelia looked disappointed. "Don't say no.
Keep your promise, Simon."

It seemed he could deny her nothing. He hesitated, then released the top button near the collar. Her eyes widened, but she
said nothing as he freed the others. Reminding himself that he
was only baring his chest—something that most English men
and women wouldn't think twice about—he pushed the fabric
off his shoulders.

When his shirt was crumpled in his hands, he waited for
her to look her fill. When she craned her neck, he turned so
she could see the tattoos decorating his shoulders and upper
back.

After a long moment, she nodded. "*Danke.*"

Feeling exposed, he shook out the shirt and slipped it back on.

Once almost all the buttons were fastened, he made himself
meet her eyes. "Are you shocked?"

She tilted her head to one side. "Do you want me to be?"

"*Nee*. Well, maybe."

"All I feel is disappointment."

"Because I damaged my skin?"

She laughed softly. "Not at all. I'm simply disappointed that you came to spend time with me all those afternoons but you never told me anything about your past . . . or showed me those tattoos."

He felt a pinch in his spine. That bit of pain reminded him that speaking of his past was only going to bring pain and remorse. "I just did." He reached for her hand. "Now, can we talk about us?"

After a lengthy pause she said, "Simon, right now there is no 'us.'"

He rolled down his sleeve and buttoned the cuff. "You're still not going to let me back into your good graces? Not even after I took off my shirt?"

"Come now. I have two brothers. Your decorated bare chest wasn't all that shocking."

He'd thought it was. He'd thought showing her the tattoos he'd tried so hard to keep from her view was almost as revealing as if he'd opened up his soul to her. "I don't know what else you want from me. I showed you my tattoos and told you about my siblings. I even talked about prison."

Staring at him quietly, she whispered, "I think there's more."

"I'm not going to take my pants off, too. There ain't no more tattoos to discover."

To his surprise, she smiled. "I'm not hunting for tattoos, Simon. I'm hunting for more secrets."

He broke out in a cold sweat. "I can't tell you all my secrets.

I'm sorry, but I canna talk about what happened at my parents' house. Not yet."

At last she slipped her hand in his. "All right. Not yet."

"I'm not giving up on us, Amelia."

For a split second, he could have sworn he spied relief in her eyes. "I will see you soon, then."

"*Jah*. You will. Now I'm going to go out to the barn and check on that silly goat of yours. After I make sure she's as happy as she can be while hungering for you, I'll leave."

Her lips almost twitched. "*Danke* for checking on Princess."

Unable to help himself, he reached out and cradled her cheek in his palm. Allowed his rough fingertips to brush against her soft skin, feel the warmth that she always gave him. It might have been his imagination, but he thought she pressed her cheek against his hand. Almost as if she, too, was seeking his touch.

Encouraged, he got on one knee and moved closer. Allowed his lips to brush against the tender skin of her ear. "Hey, Amelia?"

She trembled. "*Jah?*"

"Don't let Pierce call on you anymore. Or that man from Millersburg."

"His name was Benjamin."

Smiling against the nape of her neck, he whispered, "It don't matter. You won't be needin' to see him again."

"*Nee?*"

"No. You see, I'm courting you now. Just me."

"Hmm."

Feeling like he needed to make her understand, he said, "You won't regret this, Amelia. You see, no one will care for you like I do. No one."

"All right, Simon," she said at last, her voice breathless. "From now on, there is no one but you."

After pressing his lips to the spot where her pulse was racing on her neck, he got to his feet. "*Danke*, Amelia." He nodded, then turned.

Only when he was halfway to the barn and out of sight did he smile. At last, she was his.

Chapter 17

Friday, October 16

Two days had passed since Simon had come over and reclaimed her heart.

Every time Amelia thought of the things he'd told her, of the things he'd revealed, her heart would beat a little quicker and she'd feel warm inside. Though she'd been infatuated with Simon for the majority of her life, she hadn't been prepared for how much his devotion would affect her. She was both dying to share the things he'd said with Rebecca and needing to keep everything that had happened between them to herself in case he changed his mind again.

He'd come the next night, too. However, this time, he'd sat across from her very properly and talked about work. She'd made him laugh when she shared a story about Princess eating Lukas's new straw hat. Their conversation had been sweet and simple, nothing like the intense, heated one the night before.

Tonight, Simon couldn't come over because Rebecca and

Darla had planned a family supper. Though she'd at first been disappointed to not see Simon, Amelia knew it was good for them to take a small break, too. More than anything, they needed time to adjust to their new relationship.

Now Lukas helped her to her seat at the table. After being the center of so much drama, she was content to be an observer. And there was certainly a lot to observe!

Rebecca and Jacob and Lilly and Oscar, the bulldog puppy, were over. So was Peter, Lilly's beau. He kept staring at Lilly while pretending not to. As for Lilly? Well, she blushed a lot.

Rebecca kept staring at Jacob with a smile on her face and was watching Lilly and Peter with a look of soft encouragement.

Evan and Samuel, Darla's younger twin brothers, were in attendance, too. They kept everyone laughing with stories about attempting to help tourists at the lumber mill's retail store.

The meal was as wonderful as the people who surrounded it. Darla and Rebecca had made a platter of fried chicken, a pot of chili, cornbread, green salad, pumpkin bars, and monster cookies.

In fact, the only person at the table who didn't seem relaxed and happy was Lukas. He kept staring at the front door like he was afraid an intruder was going to burst inside and rob them all.

Then, just as supper was winding down, they all heard a clatter at the door before it opened slowly.

Then Amelia saw him.

"Levi!" she called out.

"Hey, Amy," he said softly.

Before she could reply, tears threatened to fall. Oh, but he looked so good. Tan and fit. He seemed bigger, more muscular. Healthy. But what mattered the most was his expression. He looked happy and at peace—as if all the demons he'd been fighting before his departure had fled. She was so relieved and thankful, she stopped trying to hold back those tears.

She cried openly as the rest of the family gathered around him. Hugs were exchanged, along with gentle teasing and exclamations about how long it had been . . . and how different everyone looked.

Rebecca introduced her husband to Levi. They shook hands.

Hampered by her cast, Amelia stayed in her chair and looked on. For the first time in several long months, they were all together again. Lukas, so strong and stalwart. Rebecca, so bossy and yet so tenderhearted. And Levi. Brash, handsome, intense Levi. And her, of course.

Levi made the four of them a complete unit. A family again.

She'd gotten her wish. Lukas had listened to her and given her this gift. That was enough. At that moment, she knew she owed Lukas a lot. He'd done this for her.

She'd just swiped her eyes with a paper napkin when Levi turned to her and smiled. "Has it been so long that you don't feel the need to come tell me hello, Amy?"

She kicked out her cast-covered leg. "I still need crutches. I thought I'd simply wait until you had time for me."

Something flickered in his eyes as he broke apart from the rest of the family and walked to her side. Bending down slightly, he held out his arms. "Come here," he said as he gripped her under her arms and pulled her to her feet, just like he used to do when they were teenagers and he'd already surpassed her height by four or five inches.

Of course, now he was stronger. She held on tight and buried her face in his neck. He smelled like he always did. Of sunshine and happiness and grass.

After squeezing her tight, he released her and helped her sit back down. "You okay?"

"I'm better now." Looking at the rest of the family who had grown suspiciously silent, she raised her voice. "Levi, you always did know how to make an entrance."

He laughed. "One learns to stand out in this bunch."

Rebecca set a place for Levi at the table. Samuel brought in another chair from the kitchen, depositing it between them.

Holding out a plate, Darla asked sweetly, "Are you hungry, Levi?"

He grinned. "Absolutely."

After taking his seat, he began serving himself from the many dishes scattered on the table. The twins helped, passing him a bowl of chili topped with cheddar cheese and onions. When at last Levi's plate was filled, he bowed his head and gave thanks before diving in.

After giving him time to have a few bites, Samuel blurted, "Levi, where've you been?"

"Down in Florida."

"Where in Florida?" Evan asked.

"Pinecraft."

"Which explains your tan," Amelia said.

"I've been doing construction."

Jacob grinned. "I spent most of my life working construction outside in the Florida sun. How did you find it?"

"Hot," Levi replied. "But good."

"You look like you put on twenty pounds of muscle," Lukas said.

"I might have," Levi replied as he speared another piece of chicken. "I worked hard."

After Rebecca passed him two piping-hot cornbread muffins, he smiled. "*Danke,* Becky. This meal is wonderful-*gut.*"

"I can't take all the credit. Darla did most of the cooking."

Tension filled the air as each of them no doubt remembered how upset Levi had been by Lukas's and Darla's courtship. Lukas straightened in his chair, looking ready to shield her from any caustic comments.

But instead of looking angry, Levi turned to her and smiled. "Darla, welcome to the family. Lukas is a lucky man."

"*Danke,*" she said.

And with that, everyone relaxed. Lukas reached out and squeezed Darla's hand. "It's *gut* you are back, *bruder.* You were missed."

"I missed being here. I've got a lot to make up for." Looking at Rebecca, Levi winked. "I've even got a brother-in-law. I can't wait to get to know you, Jacob." Eyes twinkling, he added, "I'm looking forward to knowing all of you. Even Oscar."

Rebecca frowned. "You sound awfully well-informed, considering you've been gone so long."

"To be sure. I've been gone too long but not completely out of pocket. Lukas wrote me a couple of letters."

Rebecca stiffened. "He wrote to you? He knew where you were?"

When Rebecca looked ready to give him an earful, Lukas held up two hands in defense. "No need to yell at me, sister. Amelia already has."

"Don't sound so aggrieved, Lukas," Rebecca retorted. "You deserve to be chewed on and deserve to take it without complaining, too. I've been worried sick about Levi."

"Settle down, Beck."

"Oh, no you don't. Don't scowl at me like I burned your toast."

While the new members gathered around the table looked at each other in confusion, the four siblings laughed, Amelia most of all. She'd needed this more than she'd realized. It was so good to be all together again. At last, she felt whole.

IT WAS WELL after ten when Levi opened the back door to the three-season room.

Lukas had been waiting for him. He knew the two of them needed to talk in private. From the moment Levi had arrived, his little brother had been treated like a long-lost hero. He'd shared stories about working construction in Pinecraft. He'd told an amusing tale about getting stung by both a jellyfish and two bees in one day. They'd all laughed, and little by little, the strain around Levi's eyes had dissipated.

Amelia had been right; Levi needed to come home. His dry sense of humor filled the gaps left by Rebecca, Amelia, and himself. It seemed Levi would always act as the fourth leg on the rickety, worn table that was their family. They could remain upright, but it hadn't been easy to carefully balance both company and family needs.

After supper, they'd spent another hour in the living room, catching up. Levi moved from group to group, having brief, private conversations with each of them. Finally, when the hour grew late, Rebecca, Jacob, Lilly, and Peter headed back to their farm. Then Lukas and Darla rode with Samuel and Evan to Darla's old farm. Now that Amelia was doing better and Levi had arrived, Darla had decided to spend a couple of days with her siblings. Gretel and Maisie enjoyed having her around and Patsy always appreciated the help.

Sometimes, Lukas stayed the night there, too. But with Amelia unable to do chores and Levi just back, this wasn't the right time.

When Lukas got home after dropping off Darla, he heard Levi and Amelia talking in her room. A few moments later, he heard Levi walk down the stairs and head outside. Knowing Levi likely needed some time to himself, Lukas finished cleaning up the kitchen. Then he sat down to wait for his brother in the three-season room.

It was a place none of them ever used. He usually didn't feel comfortable there because it had been their mother's favorite room in the house. She'd quilted and sewed in there. If Lukas tried real hard, he could still hear her soft, melodic voice drifting through the air. She'd loved to hum and talk and tell stories and laugh. Daed had often said the silence had been the hardest thing to get used to after she'd gone to Heaven.

Lukas was just allowing himself to wonder what their lives would be like if she were still living when Levi sat down in their mother's old rocking chair.

"Why are you in here?" he asked, taking an experimental rock.

Lukas shrugged. "Don't know. I guess it felt like as good a place as any."

Levi rocked again. "Maybe so. I don't really remember Mamm, but I remember her sitting in here."

"I was just thinking about that." Needing to change the subject, he said, "Did you have a good talk with Amy?"

Levi nodded. He took a big gulp of water from the Mason jar that Lukas hadn't even been aware he was holding. "She seems all right. I wasn't sure if she was going to be mad at me for leaving or not."

"You came at the right time. She's happy again."

"What do you mean by that? Was she really that upset with me for leaving?"

"She was disappointed that you left, but lately she and I have been going round and round. She hasn't been all that happy with me. Like I told you after supper, I made a mess of things with Simon Hochstetler. I refused to hold my tongue." Grimacing, he added, "And I paid the price for that."

"You had every right to voice your concerns. Simon ain't exactly a poster child for proper behavior."

"That's true. But then again, I don't think any of us are."

Levi laughed. "You're right. I, of all people, need to stop casting stones."

There was something in his brother's tone that struck Lukas as new. He wondered if Levi had been through a whole lot more in Florida than he was letting on. But now wasn't the right time to pry into Levi's secrets, not until he shared a couple of his own.

Though it hurt to be so vulnerable, he continued. "At first, I didn't think Amelia was ever going to forgive me."

"She ain't the type to hold a grudge."

Remembering the hurt in her eyes, Lukas shook his head. "She did a pretty fair job of holding on to this one. I deserved it, too. I interfered and said some horrible things to Simon."

"We all have said and done things we regret." Lightening his tone, he added, "Why, Rebecca's done that her whole life!"

Lukas grinned. "You have a point there."

"Amelia ain't perfect. I think she felt badly for giving you the cold shoulder."

"Perhaps."

"Come on. I'm sure even our father sometimes blurted things he wished he hadn't."

Lukas blinked, then chuckled as a memory so stark and vivid it could have happened just yesterday came to mind. "Hey, remember when he forgot Rebecca's birthday?"

Levi ran a hand through his hair. "If he was alive, Becky would still be bringing that up. *Nee,* I was thinking about when Daed hired that fool from Michigan who couldn't tell a post from a toothpick."

Lukas laughed. "He was working for Simon. I thought Simon was going to kill him at least once a week."

"And no matter how many times you or I or Simon tried to tell our father that Greg needed to be fired, he would say we were being too hard on him."

"You're right. He wouldn't listen to a word we said, until he walked in and witnessed Greg lazing about and complaining . . . about him!"

Levi grinned. "He was out the next day. An hour later, I think the men in Warehouse Three were practically throwing a party."

Lukas leaned back against the cushions of the couch. He doubted he'd been so relaxed in weeks. "What do you want to do now? I saw that you brought home all your belongings, so I'm guessing that you want to stay."

"I do."

He was so relieved, Lukas felt like raising his hand in triumph. But after assuming too much with Amelia, he didn't expect Levi would want to continue with how things had always been. "Do . . . do you still want to work at the mill?"

"Of course." After a pause, worry filled his brown eyes. "You want me there, don't you?"

"Of course I do." Unable to hold back the emotion in his voice, he said, "You're as much a part of Kinsinger Lumber as I am, brother. I can't wait for you to start."

Levi exhaled. After a pause, he said, "I thought maybe I'd spend the rest of the week here with Amelia. You know, help her out when I can. And make sure she doesn't have to deal with any more surprise callers."

"You heard about them?"

"*Jah.*" He rolled his eyes. "That Benjamin sounded way too pushy, and Pierce? He's an idiot. Like Amy wants to be around a mess of goats all day."

"Did you talk to her about Simon?"

"Not really. It might take a while, but they're going to figure things out. They're meant to be together. They kind of always were."

"You sound so sure." How could his little brother be so sure? "She hasn't been making things easy for him."

"Good. She's got some pride, of course. But Simon will climb whatever obstacle she puts in front of him. He loves her."

"She knows about his past now."

"She knows he's a good man, Lukas. And what's more, you and I both know he is, too. There is not another man in the county who will love Amelia like he does. He adores her."

"Darla said the same." When he noticed Levi tense, he said, "Do we need to talk about Darla and her siblings?"

"*Nee.*" Shifting uncomfortably, he added, "Simon ain't the only person who has grown and changed recently. I learned a couple of things about paying dues and fresh starts after I left here."

"Want to talk about it?"

"Definitely not." Staring at him hard, he said, "Just know this. I don't want to fight with you anymore. It's not worth it."

"I agree."

"And . . . well, I really don't want to pick a fight about love."

Lukas couldn't resist smiling slightly. It was so good to know they were on the same page. "Me, either."

Levi rocked again. "Luke, are you happy? That's what matters."

"I am." Trying to think of the right words, he continued. "Darla and me? I kinda feel like we're bookends."

"Bookends."

"*Jah*. We're very different people and we've got a lot of people in between us who matter. But she makes me feel at ease. Whole, I guess."

"She always has." Looking reflective, Levi said, "And about the accident, I was being unfair about her father and her family. I knew that it didn't really matter who was at fault or who did what that day. What mattered was that we lost some good men and we had to overcome our grief."

"It's taken time, but I think we all have."

"I suspect so. Hope so. We all need to look toward our futures instead of wishing our pasts were different. Ain't so?"

Lukas nodded. Looking out the window, he blinked in surprise. The large windows framed a full moon and more stars than one could ever hope to count. Some of the leaves had started to fall, making the branches look stark and still. Even though it looked so different than in the summer, with the beds of blooming flowers, leafy trees, and rolling hills covered with green grass, it was still beautiful.

It was a good reminder that beauty and promise could come from even the most drastic changes.

"Brother, if Amelia marries Simon, you'll be the only one of us that's unattached. After you get settled, it will be time for you to start doing a little bit of courting yourself."

He chuckled. "I don't think so. I'm glad for all of you. I really am. But I'm not ready to start looking for a wife. I've got some things I need to do on my own first."

There was that edge in his brother's tone again. Levi had secrets. A lot of them. Lukas wondered if those secrets were from what had happened in Charm or in Pinecraft. He knew his brother well enough not to pry, however. All that would get him was a scowl and resentment.

Instead, he yawned. "I better get some sleep. Dawn breaks early."

"It always has. Good night, brother."

"I'm glad you're back."

"I know. I'm glad, too."

Lukas smiled at him, but as he was walking to his room, he realized that Levi's smile hadn't quite reached his eyes.

Chapter 18

Tuesday, October 20

These roses are beautiful, Simon," Amelia said. "But I'm sure they were expensive. You're spoiling me."

Sitting by her side, he shook his head. "They're just flowers from the market. I saw them on my way home from work today. They weren't all that expensive."

"But still . . ."

"But still, if pink roses make you happy, I'll bring them to you all the time." Looking at her directly, he said, "I like spoiling you."

"Oh, Simon."

Slowly he smiled. "You're blushing, Amy."

"I guess I am." Amelia couldn't pretend that she didn't enjoy his attention, however. She'd doubted she'd ever take his interest in her for granted. Little by little, she was becoming more at ease. She smiled more, teased him more, and even sometimes allowed her affection for him to shine through.

When they talked privately, Simon patiently answered every question about his past that she asked. To her surprise, she wasn't as disturbed or shocked by the things he'd told her as she'd first thought she would be. Maybe it was because she'd already imagined the worst. The truth was far easier to tackle than the outlandish worries she'd entertained those few days after she'd gotten home from the hospital.

What had been a surprise was that Simon was just as eager to learn more about her past. She surely hadn't expected that. Knowing he'd been close to her brothers and her father, Amelia had believed that he knew everything he'd ever wanted to know about her.

She'd been quite mistaken! Over the last few days, Simon had asked her questions about subjects she'd liked in school and friends she'd had. He'd also encouraged her to talk about the faint memories of her mother. When she'd cried while relaying a story about her mother sewing a special doll, he'd held her hand patiently.

He'd been so sweet, she even confided how she often felt like the odd one out in her family because she preferred to stay at home instead of work at the mill. Of course, when he'd kissed her cheek and confided that he was glad she wasn't around a bunch of men all day, she turned a bright red.

Last night, he'd joined the rest of the family in the living room. Rebecca and Jacob had come over, as had Hannah Eicher and her new English friend, Rob. They'd all pretended to put together a two-thousand-piece jigsaw puzzle. Actually, no one had done much of anything besides eat cherry pie.

But the whole time, Simon had stayed by her side. He'd been relaxed and fun. He'd chatted about all sorts of subjects. And he'd also been openly affectionate with her.

The first time he'd slipped his arm around her as she got her balance on her crutches, Amelia had been sure that Levi or Lukas was going to fuss. Instead, they'd acted like they wanted Simon to be attentive to her!

It had been both confusing and exhilarating.

But now as he stood at the front door, his hat in his hand, Amelia was beginning to wonder how he was getting anything done at his farm. He seemed intent on spending all of his free time with her.

"I can't seem to stay away from you, Amelia."

"Can't?"

"I don't want to, either," he replied, looking faintly amused. "Now that I have both your permission and your siblings' blessings, I don't want to spend another evening alone when I could be with you."

He was so bold! She didn't mind that boldness, but she was still unsure of how to respond to it. Biting her lip, she shifted uncomfortably.

He noticed. "Don't worry. I'm not going to push you to do anything that you don't want to do," he said with obvious care. "We can take things as slowly as you want."

"I'm not sure if I need to go slowly. It's just that when you say things like that, I don't know how to respond."

"That is the last thing you need to worry about. You can respond to me any way you want. Always."

He looked so earnest, she couldn't resist teasing him a bit. "Always?"

He laughed. "Uh-oh. You're teasing me now."

She was about to tell him that she liked teasing him when she could have sworn she heard Lukas mutter something under his

breath from the next room. Her brother tried to give them privacy, but he seemed incapable of leaving the house when Simon
came calling. Instead, he and Darla retreated to a different
room. But the walls weren't that thick, and she was well aware
that her conversation with Simon sometimes drifted toward her
brothers' ears.

It was beyond frustrating that the moment everything between her and Simon was finally coming together, they were
being observed like teenagers.

Looking concerned again that he was being too pushy, Simon
leaned forward. "What's wrong?"

"Nothing. It's just that this"—she waved a hand—"is getting
irksome."

He looked around. "What is?"

She gestured to her cast. "This. Or, I guess I should say, *that*."
Looking over her shoulder at the kitchen, which had gone suspiciously quiet, she said, "I feel like we might as well invite my
family into every single conversation that we have. Because we're
stuck in this room, we have no privacy."

"We're not that bad, Amy," Lukas called out.

The whole situation was so embarrassing, Amelia chuckled.
"See what I mean?"

"How do you want me to fix this?"

She noticed that Simon's expression was completely serious.
"Well . . . you can try to find a way to get me out of here for a
little bit."

"That's going to be kind of hard to do, considering that you've
got a cast on your leg and all."

"I know. And that's why I'm being so whiny. This couch
is making my muscles achy and sore. That's bad enough. But

what's worse is how Lukas and Levi seem intent on watching everything we say and do like we are a pair of unruly *kinner*." Glaring at the wall that separated her from her brothers, she said, "It's annoying."

"I heard that, Amy!"

Unable to stop herself, she yelled right back. "Levi, you know what I am saying is the truth." Looking at Simon again, she mouthed that she was sorry.

And then tried really hard not to cry.

As SIMON WATCHED Amelia try to contain herself, he felt his patience snap. Lukas and Levi were being ridiculous. He wouldn't mind a little break from her nosy siblings, either.

Carefully, he ran a thumb over the tear track on her cheek. "Don't cry," he said quietly. "I've got an idea to get you out of here. I'll be right back."

When he walked into the kitchen, he saw that Levi, Lukas, and Darla were sitting at the kitchen table. Each of them looked like they'd never seen anything more fascinating than the cups of coffee resting in front of each of them.

Darla spoke first. "Hi, Simon," she chirped. "Did you need something? Tea, maybe?"

"I don't need tea. I came in here to tell all of you that I'm taking Amelia to the barn."

Lukas's eyebrows snapped together. "That may not be safe. It's kind of dark out and she doesn't navigate those crutches too well."

"Lukas," Darla moaned, "Amelia isn't helpless."

"I'm being honest," he protested. "Not interfering. Sorry, no offense, but I don't think Amy should be hopping around on them."

"Don't worry. She won't need her crutches. I'm going to carry her out there."

Levi coughed. "Say again?"

"You heard me. She and I want some privacy. You know we need some, too."

Lukas looked pointedly at Simon's shirt. "You aren't going to start taking off your clothes again, are you?"

"What did you say?"

Lukas shrugged. "Amelia told Rebecca about your tattoo unveiling. She told me."

Levi sat up straight. "Hey, I want to see them."

"Not now," Lukas said. "Darla's here."

While Darla practically rolled her eyes, Simon tried to get control of the conversation. "I'm not going to be taking off any clothes. At least not tonight," he added, just to irritate them a bit.

Lukas, as he'd expected, glared.

Not in any hurry to defend his honor further, Simon walked back to Amelia and leaned down. "Hold out your arms."

"Why?"

"I'm going to carry you out to the barn."

Her pretty blue eyes lit up. "You really are? I thought you were just needling my brothers."

"I don't mind riling them up, but I'd never use you to do it. So, arms up. We've got a goat to visit."

"You're going to take me out to see Princess?"

Returning her smile, he nodded. "Come on, now."

"I'm not real light, Simon."

"You ain't real big, either." When she still looked hesitant, he leaned closer. "Trust me, Amelia. I promise, I won't drop you."

She held out her arms. When he gathered her close, he told

himself to not think about how perfect she felt in his arms. How she smelled like sugar cookies and goodness. Or how she'd been right. She wasn't all that light, but she fitted very nicely in his arms. She curved into him and felt soft and feminine against him. Perfect.

After he leaned down slightly so she could open and shut the door, they were walking outside.

Right away, she closed her eyes and breathed deep. "It feels so good out here. I've missed being outside so much."

"Would you rather sit on the front porch than in the barn?"

"*Nee*. I want to see my goat." Looping her hands around his neck, she said, "Take me to the barn, Simon."

He heard the humor in her voice. Knew she was teasing him. But still, he couldn't help but answer her seriously. "I'll take you wherever you want to go."

They did the same thing to open the barn door, except he left it ajar so they could enjoy the cool evening breeze. When he spied a sturdy oak bench, he gently deposited her on it. Unable to help himself, he brushed his lips across her cheek. She smiled but didn't say a word.

Before he dared to kiss her again, he straightened. "Okay, let me go get this goat for you."

He found a soft rope and walked down the aisle until he spied Princess. She was standing on a pile of clean straw and watching him intently.

"Want to see your mistress?" Simon asked as he opened her stall door.

Princess bleated and wiggled her ears.

He took that as a yes. Just as he was about to put the rope around her neck, she bleated and backed up a step.

Feeling a bit sorry for her, he moved to the side and let her trot through. Instantly, her little black nose went up in the air, then she turned to her right and scampered toward Amelia.

"Princess! Look at you!"

Simon rushed forward in case the small animal accidentally hurt Amelia. But instead of charging her, Princess stopped directly in front of her and tilted her head to one side. Just as if she was taking stock of how her owner looked.

Amelia laughed. "I know I look a sight. But I feel better than I look."

Princess edged closer for a pet. Amelia leaned forward and ran one hand down the goat's side. "Oh, I've missed you." Looking up at Simon, she said, *"Danke."*

"It wasn't anything." Not wanting to crowd Amelia by sitting next to her on the small bench, he sat down on the cement ground and stretched his legs. After a few more pets, Princess wandered toward the back door into the small pen outside.

"Are you happier now?"

"Oh, you don't even know. I was going crazy." She wrinkled her nose. "And my brothers? They are too old to be so difficult."

He laughed. "I don't think brothers ever get tired of teasing sisters."

"Do you ever still tease Tess?"

Come to think of it, he didn't know if he'd ever teased her. Their life had been too hard. But he did hope that one day they would be close enough to tease each other. "I don't think I've ever teased her, but I bet I will one day."

There in the dim light, a new softness entered Amelia's eyes. "Oh, Simon. What am I going to do with you?"

He shrugged. "Be patient? I have a lot to learn about being in a good relationship. But don't give up on me. I'm fairly smart. I can learn."

"You know, I probably could teach you something about being in a relationship. I'm fairly smart, too," she said airily.

He loved her gentle flirting. Pulling his knees up, he rested his arms on them. "What's the first lesson?"

She crooked a finger. "Well, the first thing you need to do is come sit next to me. People in a relationship don't sit so far apart."

Hopping up, he moved to sit by her side. "How did I do?"

"Hmm. You earned a C, I think."

"You gave me a C?" Even though they were only playing, he still felt vaguely disappointed. "What did I do wrong?"

"Well, I'm no expert . . . but if you are supposed to be courting me . . ."

"I am *definitely* courting you."

"In that case, the correct thing for you to do is to put an arm around my shoulders."

Carefully, he lifted an arm and curved it around her shoulders, shifting so she could lean closer. He closed his eyes and inhaled. "How is this? Better?"

"I'd say so."

"Still a C?"

"*Nee* . . . most likely you earned a B-plus."

"What? Amelia, what do I have to do to earn an A?"

Giggling, she said, "Simon, if I told you how to do everything, you'd never learn. If you intend to receive an A, you'll have to figure out what to do on your own."

What he wanted to do would likely earn him a slap instead of an A+. Therefore, he simply kissed her brow.

And enjoyed the moment. Few had ever been so sweet.

Chapter 19

Wednesday, October 21

Tess couldn't stop thinking about Simon's desire to help children that were in situations like they'd been in. The thought of being able to do something after a lifetime of feeling helpless was exhilarating.

However, she just wasn't sure that his barn was the best solution. It was too isolated. Too many kids who were in need would have no idea it existed. And if they didn't know that help was available, it would be beside the point.

She'd gone to bed thinking about his barn and his ideas, stewing on various options while she'd tossed and turned. Then she'd had an idea. The first time she'd driven through Charm, she'd noticed a couple of empty store fronts and small houses for sale. What if she and Simon pooled their money and purchased something in town?

Of course, their half-baked idea was going to need a lot of fleshing out before they could put something into place. Actually, she was going to have to do a lot of talking to Simon to see if he would even be willing to purchase a place in town.

But now that the idea had germinated in her mind, she couldn't stop thinking about it.

After she finished her appointments for the day on the east side of Cleveland, she drove back down to Charm. Two hours later, she was parking her car on one of the side streets. She couldn't help it; she had to take a look at some of the storefronts and other buildings in the area. There had to be a way to make this dream a reality.

Before she'd left her hotel that morning, she'd used the business center and printed off a list of available properties. There were two just off Main Street that she wanted to check out.

The first was an older redbrick building. It had been a home at one time, then most recently a little bulk-food store. The notes on the property report said that the owners hadn't had enough capital to enable it to compete with destinations like Walnut Creek, and it had closed after less than a year.

Walking around the weed-infested yard, trying to see past the peeling paint and sad-looking metal fence that encompassed a small backyard, Tess wondered if teenagers would find it welcoming. She kind of doubted it. It was small, far from the road, and didn't have as much as a single tree on the lot.

When she discovered the second place on the list, she felt a spurt of optimism. This building was closer to the road but set apart from most other houses. Looking at her notes, she saw that it had recently been a coffee shop.

She peered in the window and was excited to see that an expensive-looking espresso machine was still there. So was a long counter and what looked like an oven, sink, and dishwasher.

If she knew anything about teenagers, it was that teens liked to eat, and many enjoyed getting fancy coffee concoctions.

"If you want coffee, you're out of luck," a voice called out. "It's been closed for two months now."

Turning to the voice, Tess saw an older Amish man with a long beard. He was dressed rather somberly in a light-gray shirt, black vest, and black pants. He had a black felt hat on his head that was tilted a little low over his eyes, giving him an unexpectedly jaunty air.

"*Danke,*" she said before she realized that he might be curious as to why an English girl like herself was speaking Pennsylvania Dutch. "But I'm not looking for *kaffi*. Not yet, anyway."

As he approached, she noticed that he had a sizable limp. That limp, together with the intent way he was looking at her, spurred a memory. "Are you Preacher Atle?" she asked hesitantly.

"I was. I'm Bishop Atle now. Who might you be?"

"Tess Hochstetler."

"Tess." He sucked in a sharp breath. "Now, you are certainly not someone I thought I'd see today."

That was a bit of an understatement. "It's been a while."

"*Jah.* Over ten years."

He clasped his hands together behind his back. "Ten years is a long time. What brought you back?"

She almost lied, then decided lying to a bishop was always a bad idea. "I'm a pharmaceutical rep now. I ran into Simon at a hospital in Millersburg. Now we're getting to know each other again."

"And how is that going?"

She loved how direct he was. She decided to respond the same way. "Pretty good. Simon and I went to a cute little café during our first visit. Then I visited him at his house the other night. He made me a sandwich."

"That's a start, then. Ain't so?"

She nodded.

He turned and looked at the house she'd been inspecting. "You know, if you are looking for a new *haus,* you might want to look toward Plum Street or so. There are some nice homes around there. They're in far better shape and there's also a lot more of the English, too. It might be a better fit."

"*Danke,* I'll keep that in mind. But, you see, I'm not trying to find a home. I'm actually looking for something else." Taking a chance, she plunged in. "Bishop Atle, do you have a moment to talk to me?"

Gray eyebrows rose. "You reckon we might have more to say to each other?"

"I'm hoping so."

"Sounds intriguing." He grinned at his joke, then gestured toward Main Street. "Want to go sit at the park?"

She nodded. "That sounds good."

They didn't exchange any words while they walked. Tess was too busy trying to formulate the best way to approach Atle about her idea.

And Atle? Well, he seemed completely at ease with silence. He reminded her of her adopted mother, Jill, in that sense. Jill had never been one to enjoy idle chitchat.

When they arrived at the park's entrance, Atle motioned his head to one side. "Let's go over here, girl. We'll have a bit of privacy from the little ones and their mothers."

As Tess followed, she glanced at the other visitors. As Atle said, there were about five preschoolers playing on a complicated-looking jungle gym. Their mothers sat within easy reach, doing that thing that mothers did so well, talking to each other while keeping one eye on their little ones.

Just beyond the children and their mothers were four Amish men. Two were playing checkers while the others looked on. They all wore long-sleeved shirts, black hats, and suspenders. But what struck her the most were their expressions. Each one looked as if there was no place else he would rather be.

"So, what's on your mind?" Atle said.

Deciding to simply plunge in, she said, "My *bruder* Simon has been thinking about maybe starting a place for teenagers. A place for them to feel safe." She attempted to explain. "Someplace where they could visit together."

He looked at her curiously. "Teenagers already do have such places. They're called farms and houses."

"We both know not every home allows such activity." Reminding herself that she was the one who had approached him, not the other way around, Tess added, "*Rumspringa* is a dangerous time for Amish teens. There are a lot of temptations and, perhaps, too much freedom to explore those temptations. A community center might be a good place for them to explore things. It could be a good place for Englisher *kinner,* too. They would be safer and properly supervised."

"Safe," he said around a sigh. Clasping his hands together, he closed his eyes.

Tess wondered if he was praying or was simply gathering his thoughts. Maybe both? Crossing her arms over her chest, she bided her time, content to watch the children play across the way. Every so often, one of the mothers would scamper over to a child and gently offer a helping hand.

What would her life have been like if her mother had been in a place where she could let her children play like that? What would she have been like if she'd had such a childhood? Would she have turned out the same way? She wasn't sure. Now she didn't suppose it mattered.

When Bishop Atle straightened, he looked at her intently. "Tess, would such a place have kept you and your *bruders* here in Charm?"

"Honestly? *Nee.* No community center or safe house was going to change my life."

"Then what makes you think it's needed?"

"Because I think my brother wants, no, *needs* to make such a place. He wants to help those who need help. I'm certain a lot of teens would trust him. He doesn't try to pretend he's perfect. He's patient, too. They might look to him for support if, say, they were having a difficult time at home."

But instead of looking reassured, the bishop looked more troubled. "I don't know, Tess. I don't think it's the right time for such a place. Families might feel like Simon is stepping in where he doesn't belong. Then, too, there is Simon's past."

"Are you talking about his imprisonment?" She was a little surprised that he not only knew of her brother's stay in prison but was speaking about it openly.

"Of course. We can't pretend it never happened, Tess."

Though he might be right, she didn't appreciate his judgmental tone. "He wasn't convicted of murder and rape, bishop."

"Now you are being the one who is naïve. You are asking our community to trust their *kinner* with a man with a checkered past. No matter how much you try to whitewash it, he will always have a record."

She sighed. "I suppose you're right."

"Our ways survive because they're based on generations of tradition and a solid, firm foundation of faith. To be sure, some children fall through the cracks, but most people care for their *kinner* and want to be the ones who guide them."

"Simon met a teenager the other day. He had a black eye and a bunch of bruises that were covered up by his clothes."

Atle stiffened. "And he was Amish?"

"He wasn't Amish. But that didn't matter to Simon. He knew the teen needed to trust someone."

"Who was he?"

"Does it really matter? It's not like you can stop him from being abused."

"I can visit with his parents." He shrugged. "I have friends in the English community. I could ask a pastor to pay him a call."

"Like people visited with me and my parents?" Though she heard the tension and strain—and yes, hurt—in her voice, she continued. "Why did no one ever do anything to help us? Jeremy, Simon, and I were always hungry and bruised. We went to school that way." Remembering how ashamed she'd felt, she blurted, "We even went to church that way."

Bishop Atle looked back down at his clasped hands. "No one wanted to interfere."

"Even after Jeremy left? Even after I left? You had to have known there was a reason for us leaving."

He nodded slowly. "We knew. But times were different then."

"Not that different. Jeremy and I left and Simon had to bear the brunt of it all." Though it was her fault he'd been alone, she couldn't help but stare at the bishop. "Why didn't anyone reach out to Simon?"

"You know it weren't that easy."

"Why not? Was it really because people respected my parents or treasured our rules and traditions more than the well-being of three children?" She lowered her voice, letting the bitterness shine through. "Or was it easier to pretend it wasn't happening?"

"I canna answer that."

"I can't, either. I am as much to blame as anyone. I should have tried to take Simon away when I could. I think he needs this place, though. I think he needs it for himself."

"Maybe what he needs is for you to have it."

"Me? What? No. I was going to help him buy it, but it's not my probl—" She stopped herself just in time. Catching herself doing the very thing that she'd just accused the whole Amish community of doing.

Atle saw and smiled. "Tess, if you were to open a place for *anyone* to use, people might use it."

"I don't understand."

"Women could have sewing circles there. Men could play checkers or chess in bad weather. Young *kinner* could do art projects or be read to. And teenagers might have someplace to meet when, perhaps, they need a place."

"They wouldn't come if I wasn't Amish."

"They might if you get enough people on board and you were patient." He stood up. "Think about that. Begin wishing for possibilities instead of clutching tightly to bitterness."

She stood up, too. "*Danke,* Bishop Atle."

"*Danke,* Tess. You have given me a lot to think about. And for that, I thank you."

He turned and walked toward the men playing checkers, leaving Tess to walk back to the small house for sale. And to imagine what would happen if she did what he suggested. What if she not only helped buy it but helped to run it? What if she moved back and lived in one of the upstairs rooms?

What would happen then?

It would change her life. It would force her to reconnect with her roots. She might even see her parents. But she'd also see Simon and maybe they'd even find a way to encourage Jeremy to come back . . . if he was still alive.

But more than anything, Simon would have another way to try to help a teenaged boy in need. And if they could help even one kid or one woman trapped in an abusive marriage? That one person would be enough.

Chapter 20

Friday, October 23

It was one of those fall days that made a person happy simply to be alive. Amelia didn't need any reminders; she had learned the hard way to be thankful for each day. But that said, one couldn't deny that the Lord had outdone Himself.

Letting out a happy sigh, she looked around and smiled.

The sun was out, the sky was a bright blue, and the leaves on the trees surrounding them were shimmering in the afternoon light. Their bright colors of orange, red, and yellow were truly a sight to behold.

And their smell? Enticing.

Amelia breathed in deep. The air smelled fresh and clean, with just a faint undercurrent of smoke. Spirals of smoke drifted out from redbrick chimneys, dissipating in the breeze.

Impulsively, she turned to her escort. "Simon, I don't think I've felt this free and happy in weeks."

Holding the reins on his courting buggy lightly, Simon smiled at her. "You certainly look happy. You're practically glowing."

Okay, maybe she had been just a little too exuberant. "Hardly that."

Still staring at her intently, he said, "You're right. Glowing isn't a good enough descriptor. You look beautiful, Amelia. Stunning. But the best part is that you look as happy as I've ever seen."

"If I look that way, it's because I am happy."

"I'm glad. I think the fresh air is doing you good."

"I never realized how much I missed being outside until I was stuck in the house."

He frowned. "I'm sorry about that. Someone should have taken you out for a buggy ride days ago. I should have thought of that and told your siblings."

"You aren't responsible for such things."

"Maybe not. But I like making sure you are taken care of."

His words, so direct and so blunt, made her feel like blushing. Seeking to lighten things between them, she said, "Simon, I must be honest. I didn't even know you had a buggy." She almost said she was especially surprised that he was driving a courting buggy, but she refrained.

He chuckled. "That's because I don't have one." Looking amused by a private joke, he added, "Courting buggies ain't really my style, you know."

She thought he looked very good driving one. Running a hand along the carefully sanded and stained wood, she glanced at him curiously. "Whose buggy is this, then? It's so beautiful; it looks like a work of art."

"Marcus Mast's. It's his horse, too."

The horse was a lovely palomino with a white mane and tail. She was a fancy thing, practically prancing in front of the buggy. Amelia loved her already. "What's her name?"

He rolled his eyes. "Buttercup."

Amelia giggled. "I think I would pay money to hear Marcus coo at Buttercup. He's always so intense."

"That he is." Still looking amused, he said, "His intensity is why he allowed me to borrow Buttercup and the buggy for a few weeks. His wife is expecting a baby and he doesn't think topless buggies are safe now."

"It's good he doesn't live in Indiana, then. Most of the orders there only have topless buggies."

"I reckon you're right. But I didn't dare mention that. He hardly teased me at all about my need for this."

"Why would he make fun of you about needing a buggy?"

"Because I'm almost thirty and needed to borrow a courting buggy to drive around my girl."

"Did you tell him I was your girl?" She liked the sound of that.

"Of course. You are my girl, Amelia. You've got no choice in the matter anymore."

She didn't actually want a choice, but she couldn't resist doing a bit of teasing on her own. "Did you just say that you borrowed this for a couple of weeks?"

"I did."

"I guess we'll be going on a fair number of outings, then."

"That was my plan. You can't go walking, and there's no way I'm going to sit in your living room and have everything I do be observed by all of your siblings."

"You may have a point. Lukas and Levi would continue to eavesdrop."

"They would. And then they'd watch me like a hawk to make sure I didn't do anything I shouldn't."

She turned slightly so she could see his face better. "And what do you think they'd worry you would do?"

He opened his mouth. Shut it. Then shook his head. "I have no idea."

"Hmm."

"But because you're my girl now, I'm not going to let you go."

Oh, the things he said! "I guess it's a good thing that I wasn't too smitten with Pierce."

He scowled. "Pierce didn't stand a chance with you. When I first heard he had called on you, I wanted to go right over to his house and tell him to leave you alone."

"I'm glad you didn't. That would have scared him something awful."

"Good."

She rolled her eyes. "That isn't very kind."

"I don't want to be kind where he is concerned. He shouldn't have been flirting with you."

"He wasn't flirting. I think he was more interested in my family's money."

He grunted. "Would you like me to go have a talk with him? I'd be happy to."

"Ah, *nee*. Besides, you have nothing to worry about now."

"To be sure, but I wouldn't have let him take you anywhere, most especially not just the two of you. I don't trust him."

"I think he would have respected me."

Simon glanced at her again, then gently guided Buttercup to the side of the road and pulled the break on the buggy. Looking completely serious, he murmured, "I respect you."

Her mouth went dry. "I know that."

He leaned closer, bringing his scent with the motion. "Do ya?" he asked softly. "Do you know that you're everything I've ever dreamed about?"

"Truly?"

"That I've thought about you for years? That I've been waiting and biding my time . . . waiting until you were old enough for me. Until I was brave enough to make that move?"

His words practically made her skin tingle. "I know now," she whispered.

"Good. Because I need you to know, Amelia." Reaching out, he clasped both of her hands in his. Ran his thumbs over her knuckles. Though his gaze was intense and his words were revealing, his touch comforted her.

It always had.

His palms were warm and his fingers calloused. He kept his fingernails trimmed neat and short but his cuticles were ragged. He had man's hands. Hands of a man who was used to taking care of things. He didn't push off responsibilities. He didn't shy from hard work or even dangerous situations. When the mill caught on fire, she knew that he'd been one of the first men to run into the burning warehouse to help. That was the man he was. He rushed into danger without a thought for the consequences.

That was no doubt one of the reasons that he'd fought on the streets and hung out with dangerous people and didn't try to get out of going to prison. Simon didn't run.

He hadn't even stayed away after he'd gotten out of prison. He'd come back to Charm and practically dared everyone to say he didn't have every right to be there.

"Amy?"

Startled, she lifted her chin. *"Jah?"*

"If I kiss you, would you get mad?"

His eyes had turned, changing the hazel into something darker and even more compelling. Right then and there, she knew she couldn't have refused him even if she wanted to.

She definitely didn't want to.

"I won't get mad."

He leaned closer, rubbed his thumbs along the tops of her hands. "Sure?" he breathed. "I don't want to rush you. I really don't want to scare you away, now that I've just gotten you."

He wasn't rushing her. She'd felt as if she'd been waiting for this moment for years.

She hadn't been kissed before. She knew Rebecca had kissed some boy on a dare when she was a teenager, but Amelia had always felt too awkward to do anything like that.

Besides, both Lukas and Levi had always acted as if she was someone to watch over. She already felt bad that her three siblings had felt that she needed special attention because of their mother's passing. She hadn't wanted to give them more reasons to hover.

Later on, she'd only wanted one person's attentions. And he'd been aloof and careful.

But now he was here. Holding her hands and gazing at her as if she was the most perfect thing in his life.

Maybe she was. After all, he was the most perfect thing in hers.

"Just kiss me, Simon. If you please."

She thought he might wait. Hesitate. Maybe ask if she was sure again. Instead, her words seemed to have pulled down the last remaining barriers between what he wanted and what he felt he should have. Because, next thing she knew, Simon had curved his hands around her face, leaned close, and pressed his lips against hers.

It wasn't particularly gentle. It definitely wasn't tentative.

Instead, it was everything that she knew Simon to be. And everything she'd ever imagined.

Wanting to be closer, she relaxed against him and almost smiled when he made some noise in the back of his throat and kissed her again.

Time really did seem to stand still. All the pain that they'd both endured, all the time each had spent worrying about other things, worrying about their futures . . . it ceased to exist. Instead, all that mattered was that very moment. There in Simon's arms. At last. Feeling his strength. Enjoying his passion. Knowing that everything she'd hoped would happen was happening right then.

Sometimes reality so far surpassed mere dreams that it took her off guard.

When he at last pulled away, Simon was breathing hard. She was trembling. Unable to stop herself, she pressed her fingertips to her lips.

He watched her, then quickly averted his eyes.

"You okay?" he said at last, his voice gravelly.

"Oh, yes."

That brought new warmth to his eyes. He chuckled. "I think it would be best if we continued this drive."

Just as he was about to lift up the brake, she said, "That was worth waiting for, Simon."

"It was, indeed."

She'd been talking about her first kiss, of course. What was he referring to? For an instant, she considered asking, then decided she didn't need to know. It didn't really matter, anyway. Not in the slightest.

Buttercup clip-clopped along. Neither she nor Simon said another word for several long minutes. She was glad for the reprieve in conversation. She needed time to think about what had just happened . . . and what she hoped would happen in their future.

Then he looked her way. "Amelia, say I may take you out for another drive tomorrow. Don't make me wait."

His voice was smooth, yet infused with something forceful. Intense. It made her feel wanted and fluttery.

Almost breathless. "I'm not going to make you wait. Not anymore." She braced herself, half expecting him to say something cocky. Half expecting him to promise that he wouldn't pull over and kiss her senseless again.

But instead, he released a ragged sigh.

That was all she needed to be sure that what was happening was just as important to him as it was to her.

Chapter 21

Saturday, November 7

D*anke* for breakfast," Simon told Tess. "It was *gut*."
Smiling at her brother, Tess laughed. "It was better than that. It was wonderful-*gut*." She'd picked him up at seven that morning and drove him over to Walnut Creek. There, they'd eaten Der Dutchman's famous breakfast buffet. She'd somehow managed to eat eggs, sausage, biscuits and gravy, and two cinnamon rolls. Two! "Of course, I'm going to have to run five miles tonight."

He grinned. "I'll think of you when I'm napping."

"That's the difference between men and women, I guess. You can sleep off your extra calories. I, on the other hand, have to work it off."

"Those extra calories were worth it, though. Ain't so?"

"I agree. It's so nice to spend so much time with you." After taking one last fortifying sip of coffee, she said, "Now I have someplace to show you."

He stood up. "Let's go, then."

Five minutes later, as she was driving him to the little house she'd just bought, she felt her hands start to sweat. "So, I did something the other day. I hope you won't be mad."

"What did you do?"

"I looked at a house that was up for sale."

"Are you going to move to Charm?"

"I am. But that wasn't really my intention."

"You lost me."

"Well, you see, I've been thinking about that conversation you had with that boy. And thinking about us. And Jeremy."

"And?"

She could practically feel the tension floating off him. "And, well, I wanted to do something, too." Taking a deep breath, she blurted, "So I bought a place."

"You bought a house. Just like that."

"Well, it wasn't quite like that." Slowly, she told him about her conversations with Jill. And then with the bishop. Finally, she said, "I wanted to do something for you, Simon. I wanted to do something to make up for what I did."

"Pull over."

She gripped the steering wheel. "What? Simon—"

"Pull over, Tess."

Thankful that they were on a wide road with plenty of room on the shoulder, she did as he asked and shifted into park. "You're mad at me, aren't you?"

"I'm not mad."

There was something in his voice that made her finally look at him directly. And what she saw in his eyes nearly took her breath away. "Simon?"

"You listen to me, sister. What happened to me at home wasn't my fault. It wasn't Jeremy's, either. And, it wasn't yours."

"I know that. But if I had stayed . . ."

"If you had stayed it still would have happened. Our father . . . our parents? They were determined to hurt us. They didn't need an excuse."

"I know that. But I should have tried to protect you better."

"There wasn't anything you could do. You couldn't have protected me." Reaching out, he took her hand and pressed it in between his palms. "Tess, have you looked at me?" When she started to nod, he interrupted her, his voice turning more emphatic. "*Nee,* I mean, have you really *looked* at me? Looked at who I am? I'm okay."

She stared at him. And maybe for the first time, she actually did look at Simon, looked at the person he now was. Gazed at him without the pain of their past coloring what she saw.

Simon was a man. A handsome, capable, strong, hardworking man. He was kind toward others. He was respected in his place of work, and he was loved by a very beautiful, very sweet woman.

In spite of their past. In spite of his past, he had moved forward.

"You are okay."

Unable to help herself, she placed a palm on his cheek. Just like she used to do. But instead of feeling soft skin covering full cheeks, she felt his cheekbone, framed by a firm jaw. Covering it all was two days' worth of scruff. He didn't move. Simply sat motionless while she rested her hand there.

Then, to her surprise, he smiled. "I think your hand is shaking."

Her hand was indeed trembling. Embarrassed, she dropped it, letting it fall to her lap.

Taking a fortifying breath, she said, "Want to see the house?"

"*Jah.*"

Pulling back onto the empty highway, she drove the last five minutes to the quiet street. She could practically feel him taking in the neat houses, the nearby park. When she pulled into the weed-covered drive, he inhaled.

Neither of them said a word as they got out of the car. She watched as Simon crossed his arms over his chest and studied the place.

Walking to his side, she cleared her throat awkwardly. "I, um . . . well, I was thinking of living upstairs and using the bottom floor as a community center of sorts. A place for people to go who need help."

"Like my barn."

"Yes. Like your barn. But this place is easier to get to and isn't going to take much renovation. Do you like it? I thought we could call it The Refuge."

Still looking at the small, nondescript house, with its peeling paint and ragtag yard, he seemed to study it a little longer. Then, turning to her, he nodded. "I think that's a *gut* name, Tess." Warmth filled his eyes now. And with that warmth, she felt hope. Hope for their future.

"The Refuge it is, then," she said. "You're right, Simon. It is a real *gut* name."

Chapter 22

Monday, November 9

Y ou are looking like a new man, Simon," Marcus Mast declared as he slapped him on the back. While they walked toward one of the many square tables in the mill's small outside eating area, he added, "I think I've seen you smile at least three times today."

"Only three?" Levi Kinsinger called out from where he was drinking a bottle of water a couple of feet away. "The way he's carrying on with my sister, he should be smiling from dawn till dusk."

"Does that mean you're scowling from dawn to dusk, Levi?" Marcus teased.

"Not yet. But if he gives me a reason to, look out," Levi replied.

"I've been nothing but respectful with Amelia," Simon interrupted, needing to take some control of the conversation. "She has no fault with me."

Levi grunted. "I bet. The way she floated in the door the other night made it sure seem like she'd been real respected. For hours."

Not liking the way Levi was making his behavior sound, Simon got to his feet.

As the men around them laughed, Marcus pulled him aside. "Calm down. You know Levi wouldn't say anything to shame his sister. He's just teasing."

"Hope so." He turned to look Levi's way.

Levi raised his hands in mock surrender. "I promise, I meant no disrespect."

"Sorry." He shook his head, trying to dissolve some of the tension that had just formed in his shoulders. "I guess I'm still pretty sensitive where Amelia's concerned," he said to Marcus.

"That's to be expected. I'm that way about my Rachel, and we've all seen the way Roman dotes on his wife. You're not behaving any differently than the rest of us. It's the way of the world."

Feeling marginally better, he nodded. "You're right, I guess."

"I know I am. Calm down and relax. You're among friends."

Yes, he was. Kicking his feet out, Simon raised his face to the sun. It was early November and they were experiencing an unusually sunny day. The temperature was in the mid-fifties. A group of them had taken their lunches outside, anxious to enjoy one of the last warm days before the snows came.

When Marcus and Levi unbuttoned their cuffs and rolled their sleeves up, after a slight pause, Simon did the same.

Showing his tattooed arms to Amelia had meant overcoming a major hurdle in his life. Though he doubted she'd ever think the intricate designs embedded in his skin were anything but strange and foreign, she hadn't turned from him. She'd also made him realize that attempting to hide his past was a foolish undertaking. He was never going to be able to run from it. It simply wasn't possible.

There was a significant pause from the men around him when they spied his tattoos. Simon waited for the inevitable questions that were sure to come.

But to his amazement, Levi merely stared at them with interest while Marcus grinned. "So that rumor was true. You did get tattoos in prison."

Only a childhood spent hiding shock and nervousness enabled Simon not to flinch. "I only got one there," he finally said. "The rest of them came after."

Still eyeing the arm closest to him, Marcus said, "Do you regret them?"

"Yes and no," he replied after thinking about it for a moment. "I wish I'd never been in the state of mind I was in to get them in the first place." He paused, then blurted, "Since then I've learned that wishing for things like that is a waste of time." Thinking of a phrase one of the English truck drivers he was friends with used all the time, he added, "It is what it is."

He leaned back, relieved that he'd finally been able to talk about his past almost normally. Then he noticed that Levi had moved to stand directly in front of him. Simon looked up, bracing for criticism. He wasn't looking forward to doing this publicly, but he wasn't about to back down, either. He'd wasted too much time waiting for the perfect time or wishing for acceptance.

But to his surprise, Levi grinned. "Amelia told me you showed her the rest of your tattoos. The ones on your shoulders and back."

Marcus stared at Simon's shoulders encased in white cotton. "There's more? What do they look like?"

Simon rolled his eyes. "I'm not taking my shirt off. You'll just have to wait and wonder."

Laughter and more than a few ribald remarks began flying through the air when the door to the main building opened. Simon hardly paid attention until the courtyard became quiet again. Slowly, he got to his feet and looked where everyone else was.

The first thing he noticed was Lukas Kinsinger approaching. Then he noticed that both Tess and Amelia were behind him. They were speaking to an Englisher wearing a ball cap.

Simon darted forward. "Amelia, why are you here? Is something wrong?"

"Not at all. Lukas brought me up so I could have some company while I address Christmas cards. Then, we got some visitors."

"Tess. Hey," he said before at last turning to focus on the stranger.

Then realized he wasn't a stranger at all. "Jeremy."

"Yeah. Hey, Simon."

The man in front of him looked a little like the teenager he remembered. He was wearing jeans and a flannel shirt. He had far too many lines around his eyes for a man his age, and there was even some gray in his hair. However, he was staring back at Simon with the same hazel eyes shared by him and Tess.

Simon could hardly come to terms with what he was seeing. "I can't believe it's you."

Jeremy nodded stiffly. "I . . ." He ran a hand along the edge of his neatly trimmed beard. "Well, I came back."

Indeed, he had.

TESS LOOKED FROM the small group of workers who Simon had been sitting with to Lukas to Amelia, to her brothers. It was a toss-up as to who was more stunned to be in each other's company. Amelia looked like she wanted to reach out for Simon but wasn't sure her touch would be welcomed.

Lukas was watching Simon and his sister in the same protective way.

And Simon? Well, he looked like he was either going to burst into tears or walk away.

Someone needed to salvage the situation. It might as well be her. "Simon?" Tess asked prettily. "I know you're busy, but I was hoping you might be able to leave a little early today. Do you think that would be all right?"

A spark of amusement lit Simon's eyes. "Seeing as how the three of us are standing together for the first time in over a decade? *Jah,* it is probably a good idea. Boss?"

Lukas nodded. "You don't need my permission, Simon. Family always comes first."

Tess noticed that Simon was looking at Amelia warily. It was obvious—to her at least—that he was worried that his girl was finding Jeremy's appearance too much to take.

Walking to Jeremy's side, Tess whispered, "How about you, Lukas, and I head over to the reception area? We can visit with Rebecca Yoder while Simon talks to Amelia for a few minutes."

Jeremy looked relieved. "That's a fine idea."

"Tess, there's no need," Simon said.

"Um, I think there might be," she countered. When Simon smiled sheepishly, she knew she'd been right.

As they walked back into the building and down a rather

narrow hallway, they settled into pairs. Lukas and Levi led the way. Simon walked at a far slower pace beside Amelia.

Remembering that Amelia had recently gotten her cast off, Tess knew that her brother was taking care with her. But the expression on Simon's face showed that he was far more concerned with her state of mind than any healing fracture. He had his head bent toward Amelia's and he was whispering to her. When she nodded, he wrapped an arm around her shoulders and exhaled.

His gentleness with her was a sight to behold. Tess had never experienced such care. She knew Simon hadn't, either. She wondered where he'd learned that gentleness. Had it come from Amelia or had it been lying dormant inside of him, just waiting for the right person to bring it out in the open?

Jeremy looked just as mesmerized by the way Simon treated his girlfriend as Tess felt.

"He dotes on her," said Jeremy.

"He's in love with her," she corrected.

"It sure looks like it. Are they engaged?" he whispered.

"Not yet."

"She's pretty." He shook his head. "No, she's beautiful."

Tess agreed, but knew that Simon had fallen in love with everything that Amelia was, not just her pretty face. "She's more than that. I think she healed him—well, she and her siblings. Simon loves them all."

"If they made him like this, I love them, too."

That was the type of sarcastic remark he used to make. She turned to him sharply, ready to tell him that he needed to watch his tongue, when she realized he was being serious.

It seemed that they all had changed for the better.

When they got to the reception area, Simon turned to Tess and Jeremy again. "I guess you remember my Amelia?"

"We said hello, but not properly."

Turning to Amelia, Jeremy inclined his head slightly. "Amelia, it's verra nice to see you again."

Her crystal-blue eyes fairly sparkled. "It's nice to see you, too, Jeremy. Both you and Tess." She smiled at Simon's sister. "I'm so glad you are here."

When his siblings shifted awkwardly, Simon hid a smile. It was going to take some time for them to get used to Amelia's caring personality. In an effort to give himself a moment to come to terms with the fact that his brother was standing in front of him after all this time, he waved his hand. "I don't know if you recognized everyone. Tess, Jeremy, this is Rebecca, Levi, and Lukas."

"We already said hello when we came in," Tess said awkwardly. "You were right, we've all grown up and changed a bit."

After a few minutes of stilted conversation, Simon was eager to escape. Looking at the group of them, he said, "I told Amelia that after we talk we could maybe meet up with her later or tomorrow."

"Why don't you come to the *haus*?" Lukas asked. "We could have supper together tonight."

Rebecca groaned. "We can't put together a meal that quickly."

"Sure we can." Looking at Levi, Lukas asked, "Can you pick up some hamburgers and hot dogs and buns and chips at the market?"

"That ain't a problem. We can grill."

"If you men do that, I'll make some potato salad," Amelia said.

"Darla should be home in an hour," Lukas added. "She can help you, too, I bet."

Rebecca nodded slowly. "If you men are taking off early, I'm going to, too. I'll ask Mercy to fill in for me, then go talk to Jacob. We'll bring something over."

Tess looked from one Kinsinger to the next. "Are . . . are you sure you all want to do this? I mean, you don't know us anymore."

"Of course we want to do this," Amelia said. "You're Simon's family."

Simon shook Lukas's hand. *"Danke."* After smiling at Amelia, he turned to Tess. "Ready?"

"I am. Jeremy?"

He didn't say anything, just nodded.

When they exited the building, Jeremy stared at them both. "I don't know where to start."

"How about you tell us how you came to be here."

"I work for a trucking company over in Mansfield. One day a couple of weeks ago, one of the guys was talking about Simon Hochstetler."

Simon raised his eyebrows. "What was he saying?"

"Nothing of real importance. Only that you were his contact person at Kinsinger Lumber. Then I started doing a little research and discovered he really was talking about my little brother. A couple of days after that, I decided to Google Tess. After a couple of phone calls, I discovered where she worked and got her phone number."

"Last night," Tess said, "I was working when my phone rang. And there he was."

"She got all weepy on the phone."

"I was really glad he called at night and not when I was driving," Tess said with a laugh. "We made plans to come here and see you. I didn't want to wait another day for the three of us to all be together."

Simon's head was spinning. How could so much have happened so quickly? For years, he'd been in limbo. Or maybe his own personal purgatory. He'd merely been existing, wanting Amelia, but sure he would never be good enough. Doing his best to block out the memories of his past, covering his arms so no one would ask him intrusive questions. Now he had Amelia, his sleeves were rolled up for the world to see . . . and he was standing with both his brother and sister.

It was almost too much to handle. Okay. He needed to sit down. "We should go somewhere private or something."

Jeremy nodded. "I agree. Where should we go?" Scanning the street, he said, "Is your *haus* nearby?"

Tess pulled out a key. "I happen to know someplace even better. Right, Simon?"

Looking at the key, much of the worry he'd been holding close dissipated. "*Jah*. It is the perfect spot to have a reunion."

The three of them walked down the sidewalk. One Amish, two English. Each a little damaged. Each mended and hopeful. And for the first time in years, together.

IT WAS LATE. Probably too late for Simon to still be at her house, but Amelia didn't care. As far as she was concerned, he could stay the entire night if he wanted.

A man didn't become reunited with a long-lost brother all that often.

After Simon and his siblings had left the mill, the four Kinsingers had stood in the reception area and discussed the miracle that had just taken place.

When they'd introduced themselves and asked to see Simon, Amelia had been unable to stop smiling. It was only when she'd seen the stunned look on Simon's face that she'd started to worry that the reunion might not be quite the joyous occasion that she'd hoped.

But now it seemed that they were going to be all right. It had been a good evening. After supper, Tess and Jeremy had left. Simon had refused their offer of a ride home, saying he wanted to spend a bit more time with her.

Now it was close to eleven, and she felt deliciously tired but hopeful. She was leaning against Simon's side in the three-season room, watching the stars sparkle through the glass.

"This was a wonderful night, Simon," she said.

"*Jah*. The best."

"Jeremy is kind of funny. I liked getting to know him."

He chuckled. "Yeah, he is. It was strange being around him but good, too. I never would have thought he'd turn out so well. I can't believe he works for a trucking company and has even made deliveries to Kinsinger's. He's been so close for years and I didn't even know it."

"The timing wasn't right. But it is now," she reassured him. "I wish he would have stayed the night here."

"I told him he could spend the night at my place, too. But he wanted to stay in a hotel nearby."

"One step at a time," she said softly.

"*Jah*."

He paused, then added, "I'm so glad he's okay. I know Tess was surprised. She'd always thought that he'd gone down a terrible path."

"I'm glad he turned himself around," she said softly. "Just like you."

Simon shifted so they faced each other. "I've spent so many years wishing I was better. Wishing I could erase my past. Over and over, I wished I had been stronger when I was young. Strong enough to overcome all those temptations. When I saw you again, I wanted you so much, but didn't know if I could ever be the man you needed me to be."

His words hurt. She hated that he had spent so many years filled with regrets. More than that, she wished he'd seen her for who she was. She wished he'd seen the person she'd always been.

She was just Amelia.

Just a girl who wanted a full life. Simply a girl who wanted to one day have a home of her own that was filled with a husband and children. The woman who had always yearned for a peaceful place to live and a quiet place to gaze at the stars and dare to dream about things that were almost in her grasp.

"I used to wish for you, Simon," she said at last.

His gaze held hers as his hands reached up to cradle her face. Like always, he held her carefully, almost reverently, like he was afraid he might hurt her. It was sweet, though she was looking forward to the day when he knew she was just as strong and tough as he was.

"And now?"

She shrugged. "To be honest, I don't know."

He blinked. "You don't? How come?"

"Now that I have you, I have everything I've ever wanted."

He leaned close, kissed her cheek, then moved to brush his lips against the line of her jaw. "Surely, you want more than me, Amy."

Perhaps she did. Perhaps she wanted a life with him and to carry his children and to sit with him in a room just like this when they were old.

But that would be her secret for now.

For now, being in Simon's arms? Knowing he loved her?

It was better than anything she could have ever wished for. It seemed her mother had been right, all those years ago.

If one was loved, one had the world.

Epilogue

No matter how much Amelia had tried to make it so, Thanksgiving dinner was turning out to be far from perfect, Simon reflected as he looked around him.

The dining room table at the Kinsinger house was filled to the brim with eleven people crammed around it. More food than even eleven could eat was crammed either on the table or on two different sideboards.

And then there were the animals. For some reason, both the bulldog and the goat were in the room.

The whole arrangement was loud and boisterous. Some would even call it chaotic. There was nothing to do but lean back and relax.

Jeremy, on the other hand, was beginning to look alarmed. Leaning toward him, he said, "Don't you think you should do something, Simon? That goat is about to eat the sweet potato casserole."

Since he'd been watching Oscar make two attempts to pull the ham off the sideboard, Simon figured the sweet potatoes were the least of the problems. But since Jeremy probably had a point, he looked to where his brother was gesturing. Sure enough, the little goat was staring at that casserole like it was the grand prize at the fair. "Princess does look like she's going to get her way," he mused. "If I was a betting man, I'd wager she's going to get that dish before the dog eats the ham."

"You're not concerned? Amelia is starting to look agitated."

Worried, Simon glanced her way, then relaxed again. "She's okay. I'd know if she wasn't."

"You sure? She looks a little annoyed."

"She's looked like that for the last two days, I'm afraid." Smiling at the memory, he added, "You should have seen her yesterday. She was fairly covered in flour when I stopped by. Blamed it all on Levi, she did."

"That flour mishap wasn't my fault," Levi interjected from across the long, very crowded table. "I had no idea there was a hole in that sack."

"Did you even check?" Rebecca asked as she picked up Oscar and held him on her lap. The dog didn't care for that and grunted and squirmed. More than a little bit of drool slipped from his open mouth . . . right onto Darla's little sister Maisie's plate.

"Ew! Oscar ruined the stuffing!" she called out.

"You're fine," one of her twin brothers called out.

"Am not. Patsy, do something."

Patsy groaned. "I can't. I'm guarding my food against a goat, which shouldn't be here in the first place."

"She's not hurting anything," Amelia called out.

"Yet," Lukas muttered under his breath.

While the others laughed and started passing around serving dishes again, Jeremy leaned toward Simon. "This is crazy."

Simon couldn't resist grinning. "*Jah,* it is."

"Do you think you'll ever get used to it?"

Looking around him, Simon took it all in. Siblings were arguing. Animals misbehaving. It was loud and unruly and laced with so much care and affection and love that it almost took his breath away.

He was surrounded by both of his siblings and many of his closest friends in the world. And in the middle of it all was Amelia, who was now smiling at him with warmth in her eyes.

In short, this moment was everything he'd ever dreamed of having and hadn't been sure he could ever obtain.

"I hope so," Simon replied at last, his voice thick with emotion.

Jeremy nodded in reply. There was nothing more to be said.

About the author

About the book

Read on

Insights,
Interviews
& More . . .

Meet
Shelley Shepard Gray

The New Studio

PEOPLE OFTEN ASK how I started writing. Some believe I've been a writer all my life; others ask if I've always felt I had a story I needed to tell. I'm afraid my reasons couldn't be more different. See, I started writing one day because I didn't have anything to read.

I've always loved to read. I was the girl in the back of the classroom with her nose in a book, the mom who kept a couple of novels in her car to read during soccer practice, the person who made weekly visits to the bookstore and the library.

Back when I taught elementary school, I used to read during my lunch breaks.

One day, when I realized I'd forgotten to bring something to read, I turned on my computer and took a leap of faith. Feeling a little like I was doing something wrong, I typed those first words: *Chapter One.*

I didn't start writing with the intention of publishing a book. Actually, I just wrote for myself.

For the most part, I still write for myself, which is why, I think, I'm able to write so much. I write books that I'd like to read. Books that I would have liked to have in my old teacher's tote bag. I'm always relieved and surprised and so happy when other people want to read my books, too!

Another question I'm often asked is why I choose to write inspirational fiction. Maybe at first glance, it does seem surprising. I'm not the type of person who usually talks about my faith in the line at the grocery store or when I'm out to lunch with friends. For me, my faith has always felt like more of a private thing. I feel that I'm still on my faith journey—still learning and studying God's word.

And that, I think, is why writing inspirational fiction is such a good fit for me. I enjoy writing about characters who happen to be in the middle of their faith journeys, too. They're not perfect, and they don't always make the right decisions. Sometimes they make mistakes, and sometimes they do something they're proud of. They're characters who are a lot like me.

Only God knows what else He has in store for me. He's given me the will and the ability to write stories to glorify Him. He's put many people in my life who are supportive and caring. I feel blessed and thankful . . . and excited to see what will happen next! ∾

Letter from the Author

Dear Reader,

It happened again! There I was, happily writing away, when one of my characters decided to be more than I bargained for. Years ago, when I wrote *Autumn's Promise*, it happened with Lilly Allen. It happened with Dorothy in *The Protector*. And just a couple of months ago, it happened with Simon Hochstetler.

When I first plotted this series, I knew I wanted Amelia to fall in love with her older brother's best friend. With that in mind, I figured Simon was going to be a little bit wild. A guy who liked to bend the rules every now and then. I have to admit that I was just as surprised as anyone when I discovered that Simon not only had done some wild things, he also had a very difficult past. He was different than any hero I had written about before. Really different.

The practical part of me thought I should make some changes to his character. Maybe make his past a little less traumatic. Maybe make his appearance a bit more clean-cut, too. But it wasn't possible. For better or worse, Simon was who he was.

Luckily, Amelia, my heroine, was a whole lot more than what she appeared to be, too. She was beautiful and sweet . . . and strong and a bit sarcastic. I thought she was a perfect match for Simon.

These two characters are pretty

special to me. If you have time, let me know what you think of the series and of this book. I love to hear from readers.

The final book in the series will be published in October. It's Levi's story and takes place at Christmas. My heroine, Julia Kemp, is a newcomer to Charm. She has a sweet little girl named Penny and more than a couple of secrets. I can't wait for you to see what happens when Julia and Levi meet!

Until then, I wish you many blessings,
Shelley

P.S. If you have time, please tell me what you thought about the book and the cover! You can find me at my website, on Facebook, or on Twitter. You can also write me at the following address: Shelley Shepard Gray; 10663 Loveland Madeira Rd. #167; Loveland, OH 45140. ∽

Questions for Discussion

1. The Bible verse I picked for this book came from Genesis. "In thee shall all families of the earth be blessed." I thought it worked well with both the Kinsinger and the Hochstetler families. Would you agree or disagree?

   I loved the Amish proverb I found for this book:

   Life stops when you stop dreaming.
   Hope ends when you stop believing.
   Love ends when you stop caring.
   Friendship ends when you stop sharing.

2. I thought it went well with Amelia's and Simon's story line. Does it make you think of any particular instance in your life?

3. What are your first impressions of Simon and Amelia?

4. What do you think about Lukas's interference in this novel? How might you have reacted to Amelia's relationship with Simon if you were him? What would you have said to him if you were Amelia?

5. What do you think about Tess? Do you think she needs to ask Simon for forgiveness? Why or why not?

6. What did you think about Amelia's reactions to Simon's past? Was she right? Wrong? Would you have reacted differently?

7. How do you see Simon behaving in the future? Do you think he was the right choice for Amelia? What problems, if any, do you imagine they will have to overcome?

8. Many of the characters in the novel make sacrifices for the people they love. What sacrifices have you made for someone you love? ∾

Monster Cookies

½ cup butter
1 cup brown sugar
1 cup white sugar
1½ cups peanut butter
    (creamy or crunchy)
3 eggs
1 t. vanilla
1 t. light Karo corn syrup
2 t. baking soda
1¾ cups flour
3 cups quick oatmeal
½ cup chocolate chips
½ cup M&M's (plain, not peanut)

Cream butter and sugars, then add peanut butter, stirring until mixture is light and creamy. Add eggs, vanilla, and Karo, mixing well. Gradually add baking soda, flour, and oatmeal. Finally, add chocolate chips and M&Ms. Drop by rounded teaspoons on ungreased baking sheet and bake for 8–10 minutes or until the edges are brown. ∽

Taken from *Country Blessings Cookbook* by Clara Coblentz. Used with permission of the Shrock's Homestead, 9943 Copperhead Rd. N.W., Sugarcreek, OH 44681.

A Few *Charming* Facts from Shelley Shepard Gray

1. Charm is located in the heart of Holmes County, home to the largest Amish and Mennonite population in the world.

2. The actual population of Charm is only 110 people.

3. One of the public schools in Charm is actually called "Charm School."

4. Charm was founded in 1886. It was once called Stevenson, in honor of a local Amish man, Stephan Yoder and his son.

5. Charm also has a nickname that some locals still use. The name is "Putschtown," which is derived from the word *putschka*, meaning "small clump."

6. The annual "Charm Days" festival is held in the fall every year. The highlight of the festival is the "Woolly Worm Derby."

7. The largest business in Charm is Keim Lumber Company. Located on State Route 557, it has a large retail showroom and website and is open to the public. ∾

A Sneak Peek from the Final Book in the Charmed Amish Life Series, *An Amish Family Christmas*

Coming October 2016 from Avon Inspire

December 3

"Momma, it's cold."

"It is, for sure," Julia Kemp murmured to her daughter. The temperature had to be hovering around the thirty-degree mark. Far too cold for a five-year-old to be outside for any length of time. Then, of course, there was the foot of snow that had fallen over the last two days. While it was beautiful, to be sure, it also seemed to keep the moisture firmly in the air. Now it felt even colder than it actually was.

Feeling both helpless and annoyed with herself, Julia pulled off her black cardigan sweater and slipped it around Penny's little body. "There you are, dear. Better?"

Penny bit her lip but nodded bravely. She was already snuggled in Julia's coat and her own cloak, *kapp*, and black bonnet. Actually, she was a little hard to see, nestled in the pile of clothes like she was.

But now, with Julia's sweater tucked securely around Penny as well, she had to be all right. It was most likely the situation they were in that was making her feel so chilled and scared.

But who could blame her? They were locked out of their house at eight at night on December third. There was snow on the ground, not a streetlight to be seen, and everyone around them was a virtual stranger. Nothing about their current situation was okay.

Frustrated with herself, Julia jiggled on her door's handle for about the fifteenth time. Then debated about whether or not to dump out the contents of her purse and tote bag. Again.

Somehow, some way, she'd lost her house keys. How could she do something so stupid? So dumb?

Just as that old familiar sinking feeling of unworthiness started to threaten her very being, she shook her head. No, she was not going to do this to herself again.

She was not going to put herself down like Luther used to do. She was not stupid. She was not dumb. She'd merely made a mistake, that was all. People made mistakes all the time.

But as the wind blew and the bitter cold seeped through the wool fabric of her dress, Julia knew it was time to face the inevitable. Stupid or not, she was going to have to break into her house tonight. Penny needed to get into bed and get her rest. She had school tomorrow.

Julia had no other choice.

Hoping she sounded more optimistic than she felt, Julia knelt down and pressed her lips to her sweet girl's soft cheek. "Penny, I'm going to need to look around the yard for a rock. You stay here, okay?"

"Why do ya need a rock?"

"Because I'm going to have to break one of the windows so we can get inside the house."

Brown eyes that matched her own gazed at her solemnly. "Okay, Momma."

That was how her little girl answered her most all the time now. She made due, accepting whatever Julia told her without a fuss. And no matter what happened, she tried to keep up a brave front.

Tears pricked Julia's eyes as she stepped off the front porch and wandered into her small front lawn. She had no idea where she ▶

was going to find a rock under all the snow in the dark, but she had to try.

She was not going to think about how one went about getting a new windowpane or how much it was going to cost. Or how her small bank account was going to be able to pay for it. All she needed to do was take things one day at a time. Or, in this case, one hour at a time.

She could do this. She had been making due for the last six years, ever since she'd allowed Luther liberties he shouldn't have taken and then discovered the consequences.

Still remembering that awful afternoon, she shivered. She'd been scared but hopeful that he would take care of things. Instead, he'd called her some terrible names and hit her. And instead of facing her parents and confessing everything, she'd run.

She'd left Kentucky on a bus bound for Columbus. Then taken another bus to Millersburg. By the time she'd walked into a small motel just off the highway that had a sign in the front window asking for help, she'd had a new identity.

She was Julia Kemp, widow. Her husband had been killed in a construction accident and she'd moved to Ohio to start over on her own. The baby she was expecting was a blessing. A treasured one.

And her swollen eye? She'd tripped while managing her suitcase in the bus station.

Jared and Connie Knepp, owners of the motel, had accepted her sad story without blinking an eye. And Julia had gotten a small room the size of a large closet and a job cleaning rooms. For almost six years, she'd worked there, raising her baby and cleaning up after travelers. She'd kept to herself and saved every penny.

When they closed their motel, Julia decided to start fresh. She rented a ramshackle house that needed some care, got a job at a fabric and notion store, and enrolled Penny in a lovely little Amish school within walking distance.

She'd hoped everything was going to be wonderful. But so far, Julia had met one obstacle after another.

She'd get through it, though. She had to. She had no choice but to do anything she could in order to survive.

As she tromped through the snow, she smiled grimly to herself. That, at least, was something she was good at. She'd had a lot of practice surviving. It turned out she would do whatever it took, even lying about her past and taking a new name if it meant she could take care of Penny.

She was simply going to have to keep doing that. No matter what happened.

As another fierce burst of wind blasted his cheeks, Levi Kinsinger pulled his black knit hat a little lower across his brow. He'd missed the latest weather report, but he was fairly certain the temperatures were hovering in the low teens. It was freezing and there was a hint of moisture in the air, too. Snow must be on the way to Charm.

Stuffing his hands in the pockets of his black coat, he reflected that he shouldn't have worked so late. There was no reason for him to be working past seven at night. Nothing was going on at the lumber mill that couldn't be taken care of tomorrow. He shouldn't have lost track of time.

No, that wasn't true. He'd known it was late. He just hadn't been in any hurry to go back to his house.

And it was definitely a house, not a home.

The fact was, he hated the house. He didn't like its size, the way it was run-down and unkempt, or the fact that strangers had built it.

Furthermore, he didn't like living alone, and he didn't like being within calling distance to the five or six other houses that looked exactly like his own.

Being there was his own fault, of course. When he'd returned home after working for four months in Pinecraft, he'd felt out of sorts. His siblings had continued their lives while he'd been still attempting to come to terms with their father's death. His older brother Lukas was married. So was his sister Rebecca. His other sister, Amelia, was practically engaged.

Yep, all of his three siblings were in various stages of wedded ▶

bliss. They were all smiles and full of happy futures. Then, when Lukas and Darla announced just before Thanksgiving that they were expecting a baby, Levi felt even more at odds with the rest of them.

Claiming that Lukas and Darla needed to enjoy a little bit of privacy, Levi signed a year lease on a small rental house just south of the mill. Within a week, he'd moved into the drab little place. Though Lukas had asked him several times not to move, Levi's stubbornness had come into play. He'd made his decision and he was going to stand by it, no matter how much he regretted it.

He wasn't about to have one more thing to be embarrassed about. No matter how much he hated the rental with its chipping paint, dirty woodwork, and scarred floors, he knew he'd never tell his siblings that he wasn't happy living on his own. They wouldn't tease him—but they'd give him a look that said they couldn't understand when he was planning to grow up and think about consequences.

Actually, he was starting to wonder that same thing. He'd taken to praying to the Lord for guidance. He needed to be the man his father had hoped for him to be, the sooner the better.

All of that was why he was walking home in the cold and in the dark. Because he didn't have any place else to go but work or his house on this dreary little street filled with people who no doubt wished they were living somewhere else, too.

As he walked down Jupiter, Levi shook his head. If his father was still alive, he would be shaking his head in shame. Levi needed to get a better attitude. There was not a thing wrong with the houses on Jupiter or the people who lived in them.

Most of the men and women who lived here seemed nice enough. They were hardworking and cordial, if all a bit worn down by life.

It wasn't their fault that their houses and their yards reflected that same attitude. When one worked all the time, trying to make ends meet, one didn't have a lot of time to devote to yard work or painting. Or repair work. It was simply the way it was.

As another gust of wind swept down the street, he braced

himself, then increased his pace. At least he'd gone to the grocery store on Saturday and bought a bunch of popcorn, canned soup, and roast beef. He'd make himself a fire and some supper and sit down in his small living room to enjoy it.

Sure, it wasn't going to be the same as one of Amelia's fine meals eaten at the well-worn and well-polished dining room table surrounded by whoever was in the house. But it would do. It would have to—

The direction of his thoughts drew to an abrupt stop when he noticed his neighbor from across the street crawling on her hands and knees near the mailbox.

What in the world?

When he got close, she froze. Though it was dark, he could just make out her panicked features, thanks to a bright moon and one of the neighbors' lit windows. Light-brown eyes. Dark-brown hair. Diamond-shaped face. And the prettiest pair of pale-pink lips he'd ever seen.

Lips that were currently parted as she gaped at him.

Worried, he stopped. "Hey. It's Julia, *jah*?" When she nodded but said nothing, he knelt down to meet her gaze. "What are you doing out here in the dark?"

"Well, to be honest . . . I'm looking for a rock," she replied. Just like rock hunting in the dark winter cold was the most natural thing to do in the world.

It was then that he realized she wasn't wearing a coat. Or a sweater. And that there were tears in her eyes. And though he'd already known something was wrong, now he knew for sure that something was terribly wrong.

Never had he seen her acting so erratically. "Any special reason you are needing a rock tonight?" he asked gently.

Leaning back on her haunches, she nodded. "I did something st— I mean silly. I locked myself and Penny out of my house." Her voice thickened with emotion. "I canna find my keys and I've looked in my purse and pockets at least three times. I need to break a window."

As her words permeated, something happened inside of him. He couldn't bring his father back. He couldn't fit in with his ▶

A Sneak Peek from the Final Book in the Charmed Amish Life Series (*continued*)

siblings like he wanted to. He wasn't even sure what his future entailed.

But he was a man, and he'd worked in a hardware store and lumber mill all of his life. If there was one thing he could do, it was break into a house.

Standing up, he held out his hand. "I can help you with that."

She stared at him, wide-eyed. "You think so?"

"I know so." Bending down, he held out a hand. "Here, let me help you up."

After the briefest hesitation, she tentatively placed one bared hand in his. It was small and slim. Delicate against his work-roughened palms. "*Danke,*" she whispered.

And that was when he realized what had just happened. She believed him. Believed *in* him. Completely.

For the first time in weeks, he felt like himself again.

"You're welcome," he said, smiling even though she couldn't see his expression. "I'm happy to help."